The Jam Before the Storm

Baker's Rise Mysteries

Book Eight

R. A. Hutchins

Cover Design by Molly Burton at
cozycoverdesigns.com

ISBN: 9798361685202

For all those who have weathered the storm and refuse to give up…

This one's for you xx

CONTENTS

If you follow this list in order, you will have made a perfect
Jam Marble Cake *to enjoy whilst you read!*

ONE

It was a grey and miserable early October day in Baker's Rise as Flora expertly carried the tray of still-warm scones and a huge teapot to the table beside Reggie's perch. Not that she minded, inside her little haven it was as bright as summer, so many lamps and fairy lights did she have dotted around the place – not to mention the heating being on full blast. Wondering for a moment if she may have overcompensated slightly on the cosy front when she transformed the place back to its original purpose after the Blanchette sisters' attempts to turn it into an Italian trattoria last month, Flora quickly shrugged off the thought. It was cosy and welcoming, it was hers, she was where she belonged. What did a bit of electricity and gas matter in the attainment of that?

"Get yer feet up there lass, helps with the swelling," Betty was unceremoniously lifting Amy's legs and dropping her slipper-clad feet onto a spare chair.

"I'm fine, Betty, really," Amy tried to mumble, but the words were muffled by her loud yawn.

"How many weeks do you have left?" Tanya asked, eying Amy's huge bump worriedly.

"It's days actually, ah, six days till my due date... but then, who knows?"

"Well, I've told you, you should use Granny Lafferty's home remedy. It'll bring on labour nice and fast it will," Betty said, her grey curls bobbing voraciously as she nodded.

"Um, isn't Granny Lafferty the one who had a distinct penchant for anything alcoholic?" Flora asked, setting the tray down on the table, and having a sudden, vivid recollection of a very boozy Christmas cake the previous Advent.

"Aye well, we shouldn't question the old ways," Betty replied, making an annoyed clicking sound with her mouth.

"Sorry I'm late," Lily bustled through the door, her round cheeks red and her hair flying in all directions, as if it had long since escaped the confines of her bun, "cows got loose again."

"Cows loose!" Reggie shrieked, clearly having no idea what the words meant, but repeating the phrase in excitement as if it might lead to him sharing in the feast of baked goods that was laid out on the table. He stretched his wings gingerly, the injured of the two having only been recently released from its splint after the parrot's heroic actions in Yorkshire.

"Not to worry, Sally is also running behind," Tanya said, rearranging the tablecloth where she had just pulled the adjoining table to join with theirs, "we should have plenty of space now, take the weight off your feet, Lily."

"Aye lass," Jean agreed, "do you ever stop rushing about?"

"Chance would be a fine thing, I think I'm even hurrying around in my dreams!" Lily laughed in her good-natured way and rubbed Amy's bump fondly, "And how's my little bread roll baking?"

"The midwife says he's a big lad," Amy answered, a flash of worry marring her features, to further darken the circles under her eyes.

"Not to worry, I've knitted some cardigans in the next size up too," Lily said, whipping a fat pile of woollen baby clothes from her bag.

"Aye me too," Never one to be outdone, Betty produced a basket from under the table overflowing with her handmade creations.

"And me!" Jean added, "Though my stack is not as impressive I'm afraid."

"Ah, thank you… and not to worry Jean, I think I'll have to make another trip to Ikea to get more storage at this rate," Amy said, somewhat flustered.

"Sorry, sorry," Sally spoke over the tinkling of the bell above the door, "James had to go to an unexpected meeting with the Bishop and he needed me to iron his shirt."

"My Harry irons his own shirts, I bet Adam does too," Betty said smugly.

"I, ah…" Flora began, thankful when Reggie interrupted her.

"Cows loose!" He shrieked, causing to Sally to jump as she took her seat, and earning him a "Desist silly bird!" from Tanya.

"So," Sally began when they had all eaten their fill, raising her voice to be heard above a very stuffed little parrot who was now snoring loudly on the perch beside them, "so, as you know we don't have much time left before the Autumn Festival up at the farm in two weeks' time. I have a couple of things to mention, and then perhaps we could all give an update on the tasks we assigned at the last meeting?"

"Aye lass, but let's keep it short shall we? My varicose veins are playing up and I could do with a soak in the Epsom salts," Betty began lifting her leg to show them the offending blood vessels which were poking through her support stockings, only to be quickly stopped by Jean, who placed a calming hand on her friend's limb.

"Ah Betty," Jean said, making a sympathetic "tsk, tsk" noise and nodding at Sally to quickly continue.

"So, ah," Sally looked down at the large ring binder she had brought with a small look of exasperation, "so I've been visited at the vicarage quite a few times recently – well, daily actually, by the two Vivs…"

"Why are both sisters called Viv?" Tanya asked, crinkling her forehead as she bluntly interrupted the vicar's wife.

"Well, ah, their names are Genevieve and Vivienne Blanchette, and their mother saw fit to give them both the nickname Viv," Sally raised her eyebrows incredulously, as if she couldn't think of anything sillier, but as usual retained a tactful silence, "so, ah, on their rather too frequent visits they were looking for company I think, but also some kind of task to distract them. At least, James feels – and I wholeheartedly agree – that they need to be kept occupied. That is, ah, a little job would suit them perfectly. So, in the short term, I've asked them to help with the children's crafting stall at the farm. I've already checked with Lily here…"

"Aye, that's fine by me," Lily nodded, spraying crumbs as she spoke around her second slice of Victoria sponge, "I'll likely be dotting about between the farm shop and the raffle for the jam barrel in the barn."

"Is it going to break the Guinness World Record for the biggest container of jam?" Amy asked, though her eyes remained closed as she had so far napped through the meeting.

"No, I did check," Lily replied, "that record is held in Mexico, where a jar was filled with jam weighing a whopping one thousand and five kilograms."

"What's that in old money?" Betty asked.

"That's over one hundred and fifty-eight stones, Betty! Sadly, we're just using a sterilised whisky barrel, but it'll still be worth raffling off for charity. A year's worth of jam there if I'm not mistaken."

"Not at the rate my James eats it," Sally laughed, "anyway, my second point to mention is that Phil Drayford's new, ah, lady friend…"

"The one that's set up house with him already?" Betty asked, the disapproval in her tone evident.

"Yes, ah, yes, Minerva, she seems lovely and she wants to help…"

"Hilda May told me, that she heard from her neighbour's sister's cousin, that the woman worked in one of those smutty stripping clubs before she came to the village," Betty interrupted for a second time.

Flora tried to discreetly wipe the Earl Grey that had just exploded from her mouth and nose in a rather unladylike fashion.

"Hmm," Sally took a long, deep breath and smiled at Betty, though her jaw seemed unusually clenched, "anyway, she wishes to do some sort of fancy dress parade for the children, through the pumpkin field I think. Is that okay, Lily?"

"Aye, as long as they stick to that area and don't trample anywhere else. My Stan is already having kittens about there being so many people up there."

"Has he really not gone back to the school?" Jean asked, randomly.

"Who? Phil?" Tanya asked.

"Yes, I heard in the shop that he left to focus on his, ah, adult literature."

"That's true, when he came in for his quarterly haircut he told me he's a full-time author now," Amy said, straightening her back and taking her feet off the spare chair, "met his new lady friend at a book fair in Carlisle and two weeks later they were living together. I've never seen him so happy, to be honest."

And so the gossip began and the official business of the meeting was put on hold.

"Perhaps we can reconvene at the vicarage after church tomorrow afternoon?" Sally asked as she rubbed her temples, an air of defeat surrounding the question.

"Adam's doing his last shifts at the station this

weekend, so I'll be there," Flora smiled sympathetically.

"Aye, I'll be there, veins allowing," Betty said, oblivious to the masked groans from her friends.

"Well, if this little guy stays put, I'll see you then," Amy struggled up from her seat and Jean helped her on with her coat, "though I'm not sure how much help I'll be."

"Aye, you're as wide as you're tall now lass... Seems a shame to leave these iced buns," Betty said, wrapping the cakes in question in a paper napkin and storing them safely in her handbag, totally oblivious to the shocked stares from the others around the table.

"Well, that was unproductive!" Tanya announced as she donned her pink animal print rain coat.

And wasn't that the truth.

Flora and Sally shared a look, though neither said a word.

The phrase 'herding cats' came to mind, and Flora knew she'd be glad when this new village event was over. Certainly, the vicar's wife shared that sentiment, staring as she was at the blank page which lay atop the open binder in front of her.

"I'll put the kettle back on," Flora said, earning her a grateful smile from Sally, "we're going to need a lot of tea."

TWO

Flora took a deep breath of fresh air, so much cleaner here than in the cities, and pulled her cashmere shawl tighter around her shoulders to ward off the autumn morning chill. Silky soft, in a deep burgundy, the extravagant item had been a gift from Adam just the previous evening.

"To celebrate my retirement," he had said, blushing as he handed her the exquisitely wrapped package from a boutique in Morpeth.

"Shouldn't I be the one getting you a gift?" Flora had asked with one eyebrow raised, knowing she had secretly bought him an engraved hip flask to mark the occasion. To be presented when he finished his final shift this evening, for which Flora had also planned a full roast dinner.

"Well, I don't need an excuse to spoil my wife."

And he didn't. For which Flora was extremely grateful.

They had settled into married life with an ease which had, on the one hand, surprised Flora, though on the other she had only her relationship with Gregory with which to compare her new situation, and that had been doomed from the start. Flora's father had never liked the man – had warned her off him in fact, seeing the arrogance and wandering eye that Flora had been blind to – whereas her mother had been bowled over by Gregory's charm offensive and equally strong bank balance in the same way as her daughter.

How shallow I was, Flora thought to herself, though not with the same self-recrimination she had once held. No, now she held a kinder view of her younger self, with age and time having been both a great healer and teacher. And, of course, she had Adam now to show her how things are meant to be between a husband and wife, and Flora couldn't be happier.

Even Reggie had taken to Adam's arrival into their lives in the coach house with a magnanimity that Flora would not have expected from the little bird. Of course, that was likely down to the fact that he now had two humans to feed him fruit from the fridge, but even so…

Reluctant to leave the peace of Billy's bench, and the view of her rose garden which now held only a few late-bloomers, Flora recognised the figure of a man walking back through the garden towards her.

"Good morning, Laurie, how are you?" Flora noted her gardener's slumped shoulders and sad countenance, though said nothing of either. Nor did she mention the fact that he was up here on his day off.

"Grand, Flora, grand… And you?" He added the last as a polite afterthought, clearly distracted.

"I'm doing well, Laurie, thank you. How are Rosa and Matias?"

It was this seemingly innocuous question that caused the gentle man's eyes to fill with unshed tears, which he quickly brushed away before pulling his flat cap further over his eyebrows as if that was his hand's intention all along.

"Laurie, please sit with me," Flora said, aghast that she had upset her friend.

Not wanting to cause further distress, she buttoned her lips and they sat in a somewhat uncomfortable silence until the man braced himself to speak with a loud exhalation.

"Ahhh, Flora, why can't things just be simple?"

"Well, if I had the answer to that I would have had a much easier time since coming to the village," Flora tried to lighten the mood, to no avail.

"Quite so, quite so," he retreated back into brooding quiet, prompting Flora to reinitiate the conversation.

"Is someone unwell?" It was a shot in the dark.

"No, ah well, not exactly," Laurie paused and Flora gave him the time to decide how much he wanted to share with her. At length, he spoke again, his voice quiet and hurt, "Rosa and I are having problems."

Suddenly Flora was the one feeling uncomfortable and, if she was honest, out of her depth, relationships not being her strong suit, "Um, between you?" *Of course between them,* she thought to herself, *what a stupid thing to say.*

"Oh! No. Not like that. I mean, our relationship is very strong," Laurie scrubbed his hand over his stubbled chin, and Flora let out a silent sigh of relief, "it's, ah, in the baby-making department actually."

And there she was, back in deep waters and unchartered territory again, "Oh, I see." *No, I don't, not at all. Where's Adam when you need him? Or Harry? Any man would do to be having this conversation instead of me...*

"Secondary infertility, the doctor called it. Except it's not really... secondary, that is... because as you know Matias isn't biologically mine. So, I guess it's just plain infertility. We're going to have tests, there's been mention of IVF..." he drifted off into his own thoughts on that matter, and Flora was glad to avoid a more detailed description.

Pulling up her metaphorical big girl pants, Flora spoke softly, "My ex-husband and I tried for a long while to conceive naturally, and although I fell pregnant once it wasn't a successful... I mean, well, we lost the baby. We tried IVF, with no success, and Gregory ruled out adoption or anything like that, as he wanted his 'own child or none at all.' I'm not saying testing and IVF wouldn't work for you though, just that I understand a bit of how you feel. Also, what a lovely little family you already have, regardless of how it came about."

"I know, and I love Matias, completely. He is my son, in every sense that matters to me. It's not about having a baby that's genetically mine, more that I can't stand seeing how upset it's making Rosa that she feels like a failure. And, if I'm being totally honest, so do I."

"Well, that I can certainly relate to, but don't give up hope, Laurie. Can the ladies and I do anything to help Rosa? To distract her a bit?" Flora directed the conversation onto safer ground.

"She keeps talking about getting fitter. I mean, she's perfect in my eyes, of course, but perhaps she could come along to that Jazzercise in the church hall? She's been putting off joining because she thinks you'll all be so much more experienced at it."

"Ha! Well, she'd only have to watch one class to know that we're generally the most uncoordinated bunch! Apart from Tanya, of course, who takes it very seriously, the rest of us are just there for a bit of fun and a workout."

"Perfect, I'll tell her."

"Why don't you ask her to pop into the tearoom tomorrow and I'll invite her myself," Flora suggested, standing slowly and trying to ignore the protestations of her hip joints.

"Thank you, Flora, I will. I've almost finished the annual gardening tasks up here, so I'll make a start on those jobs around the manor house this week," he added.

"Yes, thank you, I really need to think about getting a housekeeper since Adam and I have decided to stay in the coach house," Flora's brow furrowed as they walked back down the hill in companiable silence, both having too much on their mind to fill the space with small talk.

After saying goodbye, Flora popped home to grab her hat and bag for church, and to check on Reggie, before she went on her way again. Her conversation with Laurie had brought up some painful memories which, for once, refused to be shoved back into their mental box.

It's too late for me to be a mother, Flora told herself sternly, *that particular boat sailed a long time ago*.

But she was saddened to realise that a large part of her wished that it hadn't.

THREE

There was a distinctly tense atmosphere in the vicarage sitting room that afternoon, mainly coming from the vicar's wife herself. Acting completely out of character, Sally had already snapped at Betty at the first mention of one of her ailments, had told Amy to go home when she couldn't stay awake, and hurried little Evie from the room when she dared to poke her head around the door to say hello. That and the complete absence of any caffeinated beverages had set all assembled on edge.

"Can we at least try to stay on track today and get through this agenda as quickly as possible?" Sally said, taking her seat once again and wringing her hands anxiously.

"Hmm," Betty clacked her tongue against her teeth,

"actually lass, why don't we ditch the agenda for today and you tell us exactly what's got your knickers in a twist."

"Betty!" Jean exclaimed, "The woman's allowed to have an off day..."

"Actually, she's right," Sally removed the folder from her lap and laid it gently on the floor, "I am a bit... quite a lot... out of sorts, I'm afraid."

"You don't have to tell us," Flora said softly.

"No, I mean, you have a right to know, though James would rather it doesn't get all around the village quite yet," she gave a pointed look at Betty, who pretended not to have noticed.

"It'll stay between us," Tanya spoke decisively for them all.

"Perfect, thank you. Well, there's no easy way to say this, but ah... just come right out with it... it turns out that the Bishop called James down to Newcastle yesterday to tell him that this church is one of those shortlisted to be closed in the new year. Dwindling numbers, not enough funds apparently," the vicar's wife looked quite unwell to be the bearer of such bad tidings, and Flora felt an immediate empathy towards her.

"Over my dead body!" Betty shouted, causing little Tina to jump from her lap in fright.

"Now Betty, there's still time to change their minds… isn't there?" Jean looked hopefully at Sally.

"I'm not sure. There are four places of worship on the list and at least two have to go, for parishes to be amalgamated and such," Sally raised her hands in a gesture of defeat.

"Then the game is on," Tanya replied, "we won't go down without a fight."

"Who's fighting?" Lily asked, out of breath and just having entered the room, "sorry I'm late, the vicar just let me in."

"You're going to want to sit down for this," Betty said dramatically, and Flora felt an unsettled ball of nerves form in her stomach.

"I'm not sure the money from the raffle at the Autumn Festival will be enough to cut it, love," Adam said gently, after they had eaten a full beef roast with Yorkshire puddings and all the trimmings that evening, "I mean, surely it takes more than that to save a whole church?"

"Well, it has to be a start at least, it was all the group could come up with at short notice," Flora replied sadly, "when Sally asked me to stay behind after the meeting earlier I did have the awful feeling she might ask me to stump up the funds – given that I'm supposedly Lady of the Manor an' all, though I do hate that title – but she actually just asked if I'd reconsider taking the landowner's place on the parish council. Apparently Edwina Edwards, as chairwoman of said council, has been getting rather too big for her boots lately."

"Oh?" Flora could tell Adam was trying to stay interested, but the large yawn that escaped his lips at that very moment spoke for itself.

"Yes, she's been stirring things, saying the church shouldn't condone a Hallowe'en celebration, even though Sally has explained the emphasis will be on seasonal fare. I mean, it's been publicised as an Autumn Festival for goodness sakes and we're holding it well before the thirty-first. Besides, who would begrudge the little ones the chance to dress up?" Flora carried on regardless of not having her husband's full attention, as she needed to get this off her chest, "Sally thinks the good doctor and his wife have had the Bishop's ear, and have been complaining about how things are done here in Baker's Rise for quite some time. Well, if that's the case, then it's certainly come back to bite them in the bum now, hasn't it!"

"What love? Oh, aye. Why did you say you weren't on the council again?"

"I suppose I just never felt it was my place. I didn't wasn't to lord it over anyone. After all, I came into this inheritance, I didn't earn the role."

"Well, you've done a much better job than Harold Baker ever did, by all accounts. Harry told me the residents have never been so happy. You absolutely have every right to be on that parish council. Now, if you don't mind, love, can we get an early night? I'm looking forward to starting my new duties as your deputy tomorrow, but for now I'm shattered," he gave Flora a half-hearted wink and disappeared in the direction of the bathroom leaving his wife with her thoughts.

It wasn't that Flora was adverse to the idea of making a large donation to the church. Far from it. For the first time, the estate was starting to a turn a profit, as the renovations on the manor house were complete and the much-overdue repairs on the village houses were finished. Not to mention the rather large windfall Flora had received from the sale of the antique jewellery found at The Rise, and her new income from her children's books, which had proved popular.

No, Flora thought, *I can certainly afford to give back, but will they think I'm trying to sweep in and take over? Just throwing money at a problem so I don't have to give it any time or effort? Should I just let things run to their natural conclusion?*

Certainly, it wasn't a decision to be made this evening, and Flora closed her eyes as she stroked the downy soft head feathers of the little bird nestled on her lap. She had started a new practice recently, whereby she took a minute each morning and evening to think of three things she was grateful for. It normally took less than a minute, as Flora had much for which she wanted to give thanks, and tonight was no different.

Her gorgeous husband.

Her feathery companion.

It was normally the third thing on the list which changed. Today, Flora sent a prayer upward acknowledging her financial stability and all the reassurance which that afforded her.

She hoped she had conveyed that same sense of security to her tenants and employees, yet Flora pondered now whether she could do more.

Whether she should do more.

She had become increasingly less materialistic since moving to Baker's Rise, ironically at the same time that her wealth had steadily increased, and Flora knew she didn't need it to be happy. Why else would she and Adam have chosen to remain in their cosy coach house rather than moving straight into the big house, and why would she still continue to run the tearoom herself? No, Flora knew she was happier with the less rather than with the more. In a materialistic sense, at least. Yet, here she was in a position to do some good with her financial blessings.

But with that knowledge came a heavy responsibility.

One which could surely make her more than one enemy.

FOUR

"So, third time lucky," Sally whispered to Flora as Lily, who was the last to arrive, took her seat at the table. Flora spied the plate of scones, piled high all but five minutes ago, which was now looking decidedly sparce and half-rose to fetch some more.

"Perhaps if we get the business out of the way, before we focus on more refreshments," Jean said, casting a pointed look at Betty who was currently brushing crumbs from her ample bosom, and tapping Flora's arm gently so that she sat back down.

"Quite so," Sally replied gratefully, just as the bell above the door tinkled to announce a new arrival.

"Secrets and Lies!" Reggie screeched, as the Blanchette sisters bustled in out of the autumn drizzle.

"Hush, Reggie," Flora whispered, though inside she felt her stomach drop. In truth, she had deliberately avoided the pair since their first disastrous encounter, and the discomfort that had ensued when Flora had insisted the tearoom be returned to its rightful state. Even then, the older of the sisters had protested so vociferously that their venture had come to an end, that Flora had felt the need to promise that they could organise some events up at the big house to compensate. An Italian-themed night, or suchlike.

"Ah, I'm glad you ladies could make it," Sally said kindly, gesturing to the two free seats next to her, "we're just about to get started."

"Yes well, it's not like we have anything better to fill our time," Vivienne said, looking pointedly at Flora.

To be honest, Flora wasn't in any mood to tiptoe around their sensitive feelings, it being her tearoom and all, and was about to make that clear when they were all saved by the bell ringing once again.

"Oh, I did not mean to disturb," Rosa blushed and began to back out.

"No, no, please join us," Flora encouraged, standing to grab another chair from a nearby table.

"She's a corker!" Reggie announced loudly, causing the Blanchette sisters to tut.

"Much better when we ran the place, no birds allowed…" Vivienne began, only to be quickly cut off by the vicar's wife.

"Now, remember you were only ever looking after the place for one week…"

Thankfully, Rosa produced a large pile of hand-crocheted baby clothes from her bag at that moment, causing them all to ooh and aah, and effectively diffusing the situation.

"Oh, they're lovely," Amy exclaimed, fingering each delicate item gently.

"Aye well, let's get back to business, shall we?" Betty said, eying the baby clothes which were much more finely-made than those she herself had produced, and grabbing another scone – no doubt to soothe her slightly-bruised ego!

"We were just about to talk about what's still left to do for the Autumn Fayre," Jean said, nodding at Sally to try again.

"Yes, ah, well, thank you all for coming," Sally began, "I must admit I've had other things on my mind this weekend and so I haven't made much progress." If her pale face and drawn features were any indication, the vicar's wife had barely slept over the past few nights.

"Aye, did you all hear about the chur..." Betty interrupted, only to be swiftly cut off by Jean.

"About the children's parade? Perhaps we should all dress up, add to the effect and all?" She gave Betty a warning look, and received a grateful nod from the vicar's wife.

"Oh, that sounds like fun," Rosa agreed, "I'll have to think up coordinating outfits for Matias, Laurie and myself."

"I doubt there's anything I can be but a fat pumpkin," Amy said dejectedly, rubbing her extremely prominent bump.

"Oh, I'm sure you'll have your little baby in your arms by then," Sally said kindly, "and you'll be spoilt for choice as to what to dress him in."

"Isn't that the truth," Amy smiled, obviously thinking of all the hand-made clothes she had received.

"I think she knows which ones should be top of the pile," Betty said curtly, earning her a simultaneous groan from Flora and Jean.

"Pay no heed," Genevieve whispered to Amy, "your baby, your choice," but a dark shadow passed over the woman's face and she quickly fell silent again.

"So," Flora began.

"The teapot's empty," Betty declared.

"Really!" Sally exclaimed, just as the bell above the door jangled for the third time.

"Are we expecting anyone else?" Tanya asked, clearly loud enough for the newcomer to hear.

The woman who entered had thick brown hair, neatly curled under a red beret. Her face was made up to subtle perfection, and her bright blue eyes shone merrily as she looked around at the group, looking not the slightest bit uneasy at having walked in on such a cosy scene.

"I was told this was the place to come for the best baking in the village," she smiled around at everyone assembled.

"You sexy beast!" Reggie declared, flying straight to the woman's shoulder and batting one of her dangly marcasite earrings.

"Minerva, I'm so glad you could come," Sally stood

and found another chair for the guest, "ladies, this is Minerva who will be helping us with the children's parade."

"Well, I don't think we need any scantily-clad shenanigans, especially when there are little bairns involved," Betty said resolutely, looking Minerva up and down and clearly not liking what she saw, despite the woman being dressed perfectly respectably.

Even Jean seemed at a lack for something to say, her mouth hanging open like the rest of them at Betty's rudeness.

Minerva brushed the comment off like water off a duck's back, "Ah, you must be Mrs. Bentley, Philip has told me all about you." There was a clear sub-text in her comment, but Betty seemed to have either not noticed, or to have ignored it, as she ploughed on regardless.

"Yes, I've heard about you too, and your sleazy, wicked ways." Cue more shocked gasps from the ladies around them.

Minerva took a moment to sit down, accepting the offer of coffee from Tanya, who stood to make more drinks.

Lord knows, Flora thought, *we're going to need them*. The newcomer let the little green bird resettle on her shoulder, as if having him there was a normal occurrence, and smiled at all assembled.

"Well, then you'll know that I used to be Nerva Von Squeeze, famous Burlesque dancer and model. You'll also know there was nothing at all sleazy or wicked about it," she paused to look sternly at Betty before continuing, "and you'll know that I've left that personality behind, to live a quiet life in your village with my new-found love."

"Excellent, excellent," Flora said. Clearly, words were not coming easily to any of them right now. All apart from Betty and Minerva, of course.

"Burly risk? What's that then? Stripping for bulky blokes?" Betty asked, apparently oblivious to everyone else's discomfort.

"Burlesque. It's drama, music, parody. It's an art form," Minerva said clearly, and Flora admired the woman's confidence in her life choices, "but I'm sure we have much more pressing things to discuss about the Autumn Festival, have we not?" And with that she directed them back on track, to Sally's evident relief.

Flora had to admit to only paying scant attention to the actual content of the meeting. Other than nodding along and agreeing to be in charge of the chocolate fountain and hot chocolate stalls with Adam, her mind was elsewhere. As roles were discussed, Flora's thoughts were on the larger picture and her role within the village, as well as on Adam's place in it all. She knew that the novelty of doing odd jobs around the estate and working in the bookshop would soon wear off and her sharp, focused husband would crave more to fill his time.

What that could be though, for both of them, Flora was as yet unsure.

FIVE

"Flora, love, come here."

Adam stood in the doorway between the tearoom and the bookshop, holding his arms out to his wife in the hope it would encourage her to walk into his embrace.

"So cosy," Reggie squawked, accepting the offer on Flora's behalf and coming to snuggle on her husband's shoulder, nuzzling against his stubbled jaw.

"Ah, I wasn't talking to you," Adam said in mock annoyance, tapping the little bird's beak before stroking the top of his downy head gently.

"Flora, love," his voice was more plaintive that time, causing Flora to actually pause what she was doing behind the counter. The tearoom was empty after the lunchtime rush – if two ladies from the village could be considered a rush – and Flora was using the quiet as an opportunity to practice the full size carrot cake she was determined to bring to the cake stall at the fayre.

"Just a minute till I get this out of the oven," Flora snapped, immediately regretting her tone, "sorry, ah, I just don't understand how the top can be burnt and the bottom soggy. Every. Single. Time. And don't get me started on the fondant pumpkins I want to decorate it with instead of the traditional carrots. Remind you of anything?" She lifted a tray of what Adam could only describe as mini bowling balls – snooker balls, maybe? – and shook it vehemently.

Knowing better than to speak his true thoughts on the matter – that his wife's time would be better spent leaving the baking to the experts – Adam affected his most encouraging tone and said, "Perfect little pumpkins, just, ah, like you." He knew the last bit was too cheesy, even before Flora's eyes narrowed and she slammed the offending sheet of metal back down on the counter, but it was out there now.

"Yes. Well," Flora's tone was clipped, though her words slightly muffled as she turned her back on him and bent to get the cake out of the oven, "fourth time's a charm… argh! It's even blacker on top than the last!"

Adam walked slowly forwards, the little parrot picking up on the tension in the room and having the sense to fly back to his perch.

"My Flora!" He squawked once in concerned support, before tucking his head beneath his wing either for a nap or to hide, leaving the difficult encounters to the humans.

To be honest, Adam felt a bit like hiding too, nevertheless he stopped just in front of his wife, grabbing a tea towel from the counter and taking the hot cake tin from her gloved hands.

"I've got it love," he whispered, placing the burnt offering on the hob top, covering it with the cloth and quickly turning back before she could pretend to be engrossed in another activity. Ever so gently, he moved closer until they were toe to toe and he could see the quick rise of Flora's chest from her anger and frustration and hear her sharp intake of breath, "Come here."

This time Flora obliged him, having only to sway her top half forwards until her head rested on his collar bone and her husband's strong arms came around her.

"I'm sorry," Flora tried to say, through the tears that suddenly overtook her, her throat choked with emotion. She couldn't even wipe them away, given that her hands were joined in the oven gloves and wedged awkwardly between their two bodies.

"Shh now, I don't need an apology, I just need you to talk to me. You've been on edge since Sunday," Adam stroked her hair and held Flora to him, becoming increasingly concerned by the force of his wife's distress. Had something happened that he was unaware of?

"I know, I..." Flora pulled her head back to look in her husband's eyes, and felt guilty for the worry she saw there.

"Hey," Adam kissed her gently on the lips, as salty tears flowed over the tender connection, "come and sit down. Let me make you a cup of chamomile tea and then we'll talk while the place is quiet."

Flora let him lead her to the nearest table, her legs almost giving way beneath her as she sat down. Knowing she must look a state, her eyes puffy and her nose running, she pointed to the 'Open' sign on the door and Adam took the hint, hurrying over to turn the key and change the sign to 'Closed.'

"Is it the fayre? The threatened church closure?" Adam asked softly, as Flora blew on the steaming liquid in her pretty china cup.

"Those, and more. It's so many things," Flora sniffed, "all whirling around at once. I just feel so… inadequate and emotional."

"Well, inadequate is one word I would never use to describe you, love," Adam rested his hand over hers and rubbed gently, "though you have seemed very emotional recently."

He paused for a long moment, knowing he was treading on shaky ground. Adam had never been good with discussions of the heart, but he was trying to be better. He'd never had a wife before either, so he was learning as fast as he could how best to support her.

"Hmm," was Flora's only reply, and Adam was emotionally astute enough to know it signalled he shouldn't follow this line of questioning.

Nevertheless, wanting answers, he put on his detective hat – metaphorically speaking – and ploughed on regardless, "Is it your hormones changing with age?" He could have phrased it better, he knew, and Adam had no idea of all the terminology for the stage before the menopause, but in for a penny…

"Ah, possibly," Flora's tear-stained face flushed and

her shoulders sagged, causing Adam to put one arm around them and pull her closer to him.

"Would a visit to the doctor help?" Adam whispered.

"Who? Doctor Edwards?" Flora's voice was incredulous.

"Well, not necessarily, we could go to Alnwick or…"

"Look, Adam, I know you're trying to help… to ah, understand, and I'm so grateful. Yes it is the stress of external factors, yes it likely is my age and my treacherous body, but, ah, Adam?"

"Yes love? You can ask me anything, you know that."

"Have you ever wanted a family?"

"After the crap show that was mine?" Adam's spare hand flew to his mouth, as Flora pulled away stiffly, "I'm sorry love, that was just my knee-jerk reaction. Excuse my language, it's just… well, no, since I never married, I didn't think about it. I'm guessing you are, though?" The last was said in a quick breath, his eyes boring into hers as if trying to read his wife's mind.

"Well, ah, it's more of a feeling than a distinct thought, or longing," Flora said quietly, all too aware she was baring a secret of her soul that she had never discussed with anyone before. Not since Gregory, anyway, and look where that had ended.

Adam knew better than to ask if the feeling had been triggered by seeing Amy blooming and all the baby talk surrounding her. Instead, he kept sensibly silent, allowing Flora to share what was on her heart.

"It's been there for a while… my biological clock ticking, I guess you could call it… then the realisation that having money gives you a lot of things, peace of mind, security, but it can't meet the needs of your heart. I know I'm too old to give birth naturally, I'll be forty-six next birthday, and that's without factoring in my previous battle with infertility. I just… there are so many children out there needing a home, and I have a huge home that is empty…" Flora brushed at her face roughly, trying to hide the evidence of her emotion.

"Well," Adam took a deep breath, "I can't give you answers, or even an intelligent discussion, until I've thought about it. As I say, it hasn't even been on my radar…"

"I know, I know, and I don't expect anything. It feels good to have shared though, thank you."

"I always want to know what's going on in there," Adam touched two fingers to her heart above Flora's cardigan, "always. Thank you for letting me in."

Flora lay her head on her husband's shoulder, letting the tears flow as they would. The churning inside had only somewhat settled, but her mind felt clearer for the opportunity to give voice to her feelings. She wasn't even sure herself what she wanted, or what she was asking of him.

Perhaps only time would tell.

SIX

Jazzercise had been a lot of fun, mainly because none of the women had seen anyone quite as uncoordinated as Rosa. For a petite person, small of limb and stature, her arms and legs seemed to have a mind of their own. They hadn't teased her, of course, and had initially kept their humour silent, but Rosa herself had laughed so much at her own lack of agility that the woman had soon ended up laughing along with her. Even Tanya, who ran the class and normally took it very seriously, had a fit of the giggles halfway through, for which she had to stop the music until she was no longer doubled over in mirth.

The group had taken to finishing the evening off once a month with a social drink in The Bun In the Oven, and it was here that Flora now sat, wedged between Rosa and Sally, and marvelling silently over the fact that Minerva looked as polished and pristine as she had before the class had even started.

"So, ah, I hear you met Phil at a book festival?" Flora asked, trying for pleasant small talk with the woman opposite, whilst silently marvelling that her make-up hadn't run in sweaty streaks down her face like her own. *Must remember to cleanse and moisturise before the next class,* Flora thought to herself, having scared herself in the bathroom mirror when they arrived – It was as if Hallowe'en had come early. *And forgo the mascara altogether.*

"Yes, Philip was there with his series of erotica shorts, and the organisers had put us both on the same small table, in a dark corner out of the way, as if to emphasise the niche nature of our content. Didn't help my plan of attracting a publisher, to be honest. Though my whole life could be categorised as 'niche' I suppose," a rare moment of exposed truth flashed across Minerva's face and Flora caught the brief second when the woman's smooth façade fell, albeit briefly, "anyway, it was as quiet as you'd expect in our non-family-friendly corner, and we got talking. Ah, here's the man himself!" Minerva's mask was firmly back in place as she flashed Phil a faultless smile.

Flora would have liked to know more about the woman's own book, assuming it must be on a bit of a taboo topic given what she had already shared, but that was soon forgotten when Phil was followed in by another imposing female. *Was the man just collecting them these days?* Phil's own appearance had also changed considerably. Gone were the tattered trousers and faded elbow patches of the jaded schoolteacher. In their place he wore a smart tweed waistcoat over a crisp shirt and… *was that actually a silk cravat?* Poking out of the top pocket of his blazer, which finished the look, was a fat cigar. His once-shaggy, unstyled hair was now slicked back, greased into submission. *Really*, Flora thought to herself, *he's just missing the monocle…*

"Minerva, my darling," he bent to kiss the woman in question with a lingering assault on her lips that had them all looking away, as Flora felt her own cheeks heat at the display. Finally coming up for air, Phil at least had the good manners to introduce the woman who stood awkwardly by his side, "Ladies, allow me to introduce you to Bunny, our new school teacher. She and I are just going to have a much-needed handover over a shot of the good stuff." His tone, his whole accent had changed from the Phil Flora knew, and she had the embarrassing urge to snort.

Managing to hold herself in check, for which she gave

herself an imaginary pat on the back, Flora stood to welcome the woman to the village, remembering too late that she herself was clad in figure-hugging, sweat soaked Lycra, "Bunny, welcome to Baker's Rise. You'll find we're a friendly bunch."

"Ah, thank you, yes, it's Bridget Hopper, Bunny to most. Lovely to be here now that the start-of-term madness is over. Has flown over in fact, we're almost at half term now," despite her put-together appearance of a tea dress and cropped blazer – both stretched taught over wide shoulders – the woman bumbled through the words, her questioning eyes never leaving Minerva's face, causing her forehead to wrinkle.

If Minerva had noticed, she said nothing, a small tick at the side of her eye the only indication that anything might be amiss.

Phil, of course, was oblivious to the interaction, "Well, Bunny, let me escort you to a table and get us some libations…" and the woman followed him without another word, towering over Phil in stature despite her low-heeled, square-toed shoes. Flora watched as Minerva's eyes tracked the pair to a table in the corner near the opposite end of the bar, though her fixed smile never wavered.

"Well, it's a good job Betty's not here," Tanya said in a

stage whisper, and Flora couldn't have agreed more. Goodness knows what their friend would've had to say about that little encounter.

As if her ears were burning, the woman in question made a surprise appearance then, bustling in out of the cold, her rain hood clasped at her chin by a gloved hand.

"Shove up, there's a grand lass," Betty said, bumping Tanya's shoulder with her hip and causing everyone on that side of the table to shuffle further along the banquette.

Jean, who had followed her in, took the much more polite approach of finding a spare chair at another table and adding it to the end of theirs.

"We don't normally see you in the pub on a weekday?" Flora asked, as Betty shook out her curls and angled her body towards the television that was attached to the wall behind the bar on their side.

"No, lass, but needs must... Jean and I were just settling down to watch our new favourite show, 'Yarn Wars,' when the dratted tele broke. Nothing lasts nowadays."

"Wasn't that old set from twenty years ago?" Shona

asked, clearing the empties from their table.

"Aye well, it's given up the fight and Harry didn't seem to be rushing to fix it, silly man, so we've come to watch in here. Now, find the right channel, will you Shona love, and get me a sweet sherry while you're at it."

Shona raised an eyebrow and shared a look with Jean, but went back behind the bar and did as she had been told, quickly finding the right programme.

"Yarn Wars, eh?" Tanya asked with a twinkle in her eye, knowing full well she was adding fuel to the fire.

"Aye," Betty said, "it's like the Great British Sewing Bee, but for knitting. Shush now, here it is!" How the woman thought she could quieten a bar full of people, Flora wasn't sure, but she knew her friend would try.

"It's similar to Great British Bake Off too," Jean added, smiling.

"Huh, I don't watch that anymore," Betty turned to Jean, "Amateurs!"

A small smile was shared between the other women around the table, until Sally spoke up, "So, I've made a list of possible games for the fayre, as that was my task from our conversation the other day, and I was wondering if you could give me your thoughts."

Flora bit back a groan and took a rather sizeable glug of her wine, the glass emptying far too soon for her liking. Minerva, too, seemed more pre-occupied with the couple in the corner than with the talk of Pin the Wart On the Witch, Pumpkin Bowling and Mummy Bandages.

"I just wanted something other than the usual bobbing for apples," Sally finished, shrugging her shoulders and pulling a packet of painkillers from her handbag.

"Well, we could add Musical Monsters, as a variation on the usual Musical Statues," Rosa added, "I've seen that at a party before."

"Good idea," Sally scribbled it down in her notebook.

"Can you keep the noise down?" Betty asked, unduly aggrieved, "It's getting tense here, she just dropped a stitch!"

"I think that's my cue to bow out," Flora said, secretly grateful for the excuse to head home and to a deep bubble bath.

"Me too," several others replied in unison.

"Oh? Are you all leaving so soon?" Betty asked,

completely oblivious to the cause.

Jean sighed and Tanya rubbed her shoulder as they all filed past, "Good luck," she whispered and Jean nodded in sombre reply. Certainly, Flora didn't envy the woman the discussion which would surely ensue after the show... especially since Betty was now heckling the screen as if she were watching a football match!

SEVEN

Another week sped by, and Flora found herself the following Friday at her first ever parish council meeting. To hide her own nerves, she had had her hair done in the little salon on Front Street – not by Amy though, who was on maternity leave and currently overdue at home, no doubt willing her baby to make an appearance – and had scrubbed up rather nicely if she did say so herself. A charcoal grey shift dress, a string of pearls she had found at The Rise during the big clear-out, and higher heels than normal all added to the effect to which, it seemed, her husband was not immune.

"Are you sure you have to go? Can't you just send

your thoughts in... an email?" Adam had nuzzled against her neck, making Flora giggle as his actions almost exactly mirrored those of the little bird sitting on her other shoulder who was equally keen that she stay at home.

"No, I promised Sally, I'm sure you boys will be fine for a couple of hours."

Adam had kissed her sweetly and accepted defeat, but the parrot was not so easily beaten.

"My Flora! So cosy! She's a corker!" Reggie had shrieked, his attempts heard long after Flora had shut the front door behind her.

"Don't you think, Flora?" The vicar asked, his tone slightly exasperated.

"Sorry, Reverend," Flora brought her attention fully back to the matter at hand, "can you repeat the question?"

This triggered a large sigh from the woman next to her. They were rather squashed in, around the table in the vicar's study, as the Women's Institute had commandeered the small room off the main church hall for the evening. Flora wasn't sure why the women needed both rooms, but, like the vicar, she had no intention of creating a fuss about it. It was definitely wise to choose your battles where that formidable band of ladies was concerned. Next week, hopefully, the group would be back to using only the main hall and Flora wouldn't be brushing thighs with Edwina Edwards.

"It would seem that Mrs. Miller has better things on her mind," Edwina said, rather venomously if truth be told. Certainly, her expression upon seeing Flora arrive had not hidden her displeasure at the addition to the council's numbers.

"Bramble-Miller," Flora replied, her voice strong and firm.

"Pardon me?"

"It's Mrs. Bramble-Miller," Flora repeated, feeling the familiar warmth that her married name gave her, "since I married last month."

"Hmph, well, anyway, do you have anything useful to add?" Edwina asked, tapping a well-manicured nail on her knee.

"I was just saying that we need to do as much fundraising as we can, as quickly as possible," the vicar said gently, "don't you agree, Flora? Doctor and Mrs.

Edwards here think that we should leave things up to the Almighty – or at least to the Bishop's eventual decision." James' expression betrayed exactly what he thought of that option, and Flora was in full agreement.

"Indeed," she spoke clearly, knowing it was now or never. Luckily, Harry was also on the parish council, and his encouraging smile from the seat opposite was the prompt Flora needed to continue, having already sought his views on the subject earlier that week. "Indeed, I agree that we need a definite, time-critical plan of action. Which is why I propose that the Baker's Estate funds the shortfall in finances, thus securing the church's future in the village."

If she had declared herself about to commence astronaut training with NASA, Flora didn't think she would have been met with such utter astonishment. The ticking of the grandfather clock in the background and the rustling hush of shocked breaths were the only sounds after the vicar's wife – who was taking notes of the meeting at her husband's desk behind them – dropped her pen on the wood and added her own gasp to the collective shock.

"Flora, I… I mean…that's… well, what do you mean, exactly?" James asked, uncharacteristically flustered and understandably seeking clarification.

"Well, I've discussed it with Adam, and with my solicitor and financial adviser, Harry here, and I can tell you that I'm committed to creating a Trust to finance the elements of parish ecumenical life for which the Church of England currently records there's a shortfall. So, your salary, James, if that's the case, the energy bills and running costs, upkeep... whatever is lacking, I'll finance it from the estate funds. All legal and above board."

Her words were met with harumphing noises from Doctor and Mrs. Edwards, though everyone else was beaming their gratitude.

"Are you sure, Flora?" Sally asked, her voice barely above a whisper so great was her shock, "It's a lot of money we're talking about."

"One hundred percent," Flora said firmly, "and I want to get things rolling as soon as possible so that the money is in place to take us firmly off the hit list before any potential closure date the diocese has in mind."

"You can't buy the village's trust and affection, you know," Edwina said, earning her a stern "Mrs. Edwards!" from the vicar and a stalling hand on her knee from her own husband.

"What affection and loyalty Mrs. Bramble-Miller has from the villagers and parishioners has been hard earned, well won and is totally deserved," Sally stood as she spoke and came across to lay a hand on Flora's shoulder, "and I for one am extremely grateful."

"Here, here," Harry agreed.

"So, did they eat you up and spit you out?" Adam joked once Flora was back at home, in her favourite armchair, and with a glass of red in her hand.

"Spit you out!" Reggie chimed in, never one to sit out a joke.

"Not as much as I'd feared," Flora said, brushing an imaginary piece of lint from her shoulder in much the same preening fashion favoured by Reggie, "though I guess that's mostly down to the fact that money talks, as always." She whispered the last part, her smugness short-lived, and Adam crossed the room to kneel beside her.

"Don't you be talking like that, of course they were going to be grateful, but anyone that matters knows you did it for the church congregation, for the village and because your Faith prompted you to do so, not for the kudos of racing in like a knight in shining armour."

"I know, I know, and my gut tells me it was the right decision. What would the village be without the church being a church? Knowing the luck of Baker's Rise we'd end up with it being turned into a bingo hall or something," Flora offered her hand to help her husband up, "anyway, it's done now. Not much was said afterwards, but I know I've ruffled some quite important feathers… No doubt this is just the calm before the storm."

"Speaking of storms, there's one forecast for tomorrow, though the Met office website says it'll pass by our way after the fayre."

"Well, fingers crossed it stays that way," Flora yawned as they made their way through to the kitchen.

"Oh, and this arrived while you were out," Adam pointed to a large delivery box on the kitchen table, his expression questioning.

"Ah, about that…" Flora said, knowing full well that her husband wouldn't like what he was about to hear…

"It's, it's… I have no words," Adam looked at himself

in the full-length mirror in the spare room the next morning.

"You look gorgeous," Flora laughed, running a finger teasingly along the plastic hook that hid one of her husband's hands, "even better than the outfit appeared online."

"And tell me again why you're Peter Pan and not Tinkerbell? I could've had some fun with Tinkerbell..." Adam grinned, his good humour momentarily restored.

"Because Hook and Pan are more of a pair. Hook and Tink would seem... odd," Flora explained for the third time, "and we needed to go as these characters because I had to factor in a parrot! Now, let's hurry up, I told Lily we'd help with the setting up."

"Hmm," Adam said, peering around her to eye the little bird who was watching them intently from the doorframe, as if sensing that it might be better in that moment if he stayed out of reach, "so I have you to blame, do I?"

"Cows loose!" Reggie squawked, unruffled by the accusatory tone.

"Cows would be preferable..." Adam muttered,

though he adjusted his belt for a final time, grabbed his pirate's hat from the chair and followed Flora to the front door.

"Adventure awaits!" Reggie shrieked, flying over their heads and reaching the entrance first.

"We'll see," Adam said under his breath, though deliberately loud enough for Flora to hear.

And they certainly would.

EIGHT

The sky wasn't just looking ominous as Flora, Adam, and Reggie arrived at the Houghton's farm, it appeared positively oppressive.

"I don't like the look of that black cloud," Adam said, glad he'd worn wellies instead of the faux silk, fake boots which came with the fancy dress outfit.

"Me neither, hopefully the rain will hold off," Flora replied, just as a gust of wind almost knocked her off her feet, capturing her words and making fools of them.

"Thankfully, Reggie had been placed safely in his carrier for the short car journey, though his fretful squawks of "Now there's trouble!" and "There'll be hell to pay!" left no one in any doubt that the three of them had arrived.

"Hush now, good bird," Flora tried to calm the parrot, but to no avail.

"Ah, here they are," Lily rushed from the door of the farm shop to greet them, wisps of hair flying out from underneath her witch's hat, and her face a delightful shade of slimy green, "we need to get the chocolate fondue started, and the marshmallows ready for roasting. Ah, there's the hot chocolate to prepare and I must find Stan, he's gone out without his Gandalf wig. How he expects to drive a tractor in that long robe for the trailer rides, I have no idea!"

"Be calm, Lily, all will be well," Rosa emerged from the shop with Matias, who held a small, white pumpkin in his little arms.

"Mine!" he said clearly, eying Reggie through the transparent door to his carrier, as if the bird might try to steal it.

"Si, si," Rosa ruffled his head, as Laurie followed them with a box full of jars of jam. The whole family of three were dressed in coordinating outfits as Aladdin, Princess Jasmine and with Matias as Abu the monkey.

"Too cute," Flora whispered, her eyes shining as she looked at the small boy.

"Isn't he just," Lily agreed, seeming calmer than a few moments ago, "so, Laurie had the great idea to put some of my jars of homemade jam in the barn over there with the big barrel of jam that we're raffling off. If people buy a strip of tickets they can get another strip, so an extra entry, if they buy a jar of jam too! So clever."

"I'll give you a hand," Adam said, ostensibly to help Laurie out, though Flora suspected it may have had more to do with the fact that Betty, Jean and Mrs. May were heading in their direction from the makeshift car park, with Tanya striding along in front, her car keys dangling in her hand.

"Couldn't you have done something about the mud?" Betty asked, ignoring any pleasantries altogether, "I doubt I'll even be able to put little Tina down in this."

"You could have left her at home as Jean and I suggested," Tanya said, marching past them into the shop.

"No Harry?" Flora asked, hoping belatedly that by doing so she wouldn't add to the tension.

"Coming later, said he had a meeting," Betty gave the look that Flora knew she reserved for moments of maximum disapproval, causing Flora to try to hide her smile behind her plastic bow and arrow prop, "though I think he just fancies an afternoon's peace with his feet up."

"Well, we can't help the mud, especially once it starts raining, but there are a lot of jobs that you can give me a hand with," Lily said, guiding Betty by the elbow into the farm shop, little Tina trying to wriggle free the whole time.

"How about we put Tina and Reggie in the farm house?" Jean asked, "Where they'll be warm and out of the way."

"Perfect plan," Lily flashed a grateful gaze at their friend and took the carrier from Flora, much to everyone's relief. The parrot's screeches were so loud now, they threatened to drown out any further conversation.

"Any news on Amy?" Flora asked as she and Tanya began to set up the chocolate fountain.

"Betty said that she's staying at home, had a bad night last night."

"Best place for her, I should think, the weather's not looking hopeful, and I'd hate for her to slip and fall."

"All that extra weight she's carrying, she'd go down like a tank of bricks."

"A ton of bricks," Flora corrected whilst marvelling once again at Tanya's bluntness. Mind you, she did fit in well with certain other ladies in the village who spoke their mind!

The wind whipped, the heavy drizzle came down sideways, and the army of black clouds marched closer to their little village. All of the adults were ready to call it a day before the fayre had even started, but as soon as the little ones arrived with their parents, so eager and excited, no one had the heart to stop the event before it had even begun for them.

"How about just an hour?" Minerva asked Lily, "Let them feel they've experienced it, done their little parade, chosen a pumpkin and they will go home happy."

"I think that sounds great," Sally replied over her shoulder, appearing flustered as she tried to wrangle her three girls away from the cow shed and towards the refreshment barn. The vicarage family had come dressed as different coloured crayons, which Flora thought was a simple but fabulous idea.

"I'll go and check the pathway is still clear for the parade," Minerva said, skipping away.

"Is she not freezing in that outfit?" Lily mused.

"Sexiest witch I've ever seen," Stan piped up from behind them, earning him a glare from his wife, who patted down her own witchy costume self-consciously.

It was one of the rare times that Flora had heard the man speak and she felt extremely uncomfortable.

Apparently realising that the words had come out of his mouth, and not just stayed in his mind, Stan quickly came over and put his arm around Lily's shoulders, "Apart from my green corker here," he whispered.

Lily flushed red, visible even underneath her thick make-up, "Aye Stan Houghton, you saved yerself just in time. A night sleeping with the pigs was in yer future otherwise!"

Flora smiled awkwardly and slipped away, wondering how much jam Adam could be moving that it was taking he and Laurie so long. She didn't have to wonder for long, as turning a corner onto the small area where all of the pumpkins had been piled up, beneath trees strung with fairy lights, Flora came across the two men, sitting high on a mini hill of hay bales, laughing and joking with hot chocolates in hand.

Flora was about to suggest they might want to lend a helping hand, now that guests had started to arrive, when there was a loud female shriek from the pumpkin patch, the owner of the noise hidden behind a stack of the orange globes. Adam and Laurie immediately jumped down and rushed to investigate, with Flora hot on their heels.

"Get off me, you pervert!" Minerva shouted as the trio rounded the pumpkin pile, coming to a sudden halt when they were faced with a man attempting to beat a hasty retreat.

To the eye it was Gomez, but the twinkling lights overhead gave away the true identity of the man as none other than Doctor Edwards.

Adam held a hand up to halt the man's progress, whilst Flora and Laurie rushed around him to the woman who was sitting perched on a large pumpkin, arms slumped onto her knees so that her long, purple fake curls fell forward and hid her face.

"Minerva, are you okay?" Flora whispered.

The woman in question looked up, sideways, and Flora thought she may never have seen such hatred in someone's eyes before. Minerva blinked then, and the expression changed to a heated anger as she jumped up and stood face to face with Edwards, whom Adam was having to physically restrain now to stop the man leaving.

"You!" Minerva shouted, stabbing an index finger covered in a long, plastic witchy talon into the man's chest, "You think that because you saw me performing once in Paris, that I'm free game? Telling me 'once a slut always a slut!' Well, I am not your plaything! I won't just shut up and put up anymore!" She was screeching now, and they had attracted a small crowd, including Phil and Edwina, who both rushed forwards to join the scene that was unfolding.

Tears were streaming down the woman's face now, gouging rivulets in her stage make-up, yet she continued with a barrage of insults aimed at the doctor – to which she was quite entitled, Flora thought.

"Ernest, what's going on?" Edwina asked, peering at Adam's hold on her husband, then to Minerva, then to the man himself. She was dressed in long white robes, with a waist-length wig of white hair and a small placard pinned to her chest which said, 'Lady of the Lake,' presumably as she didn't expect her uncouth neighbours to recognise the character.

Ernest? Flora thought, realising she had never heard the man's actual name before as everyone simply referred to him as doctor. *Ernest Edwards? What if I just called him Ernie?* Flora wanted to snort, had to muffle the noise in fact given that it would be highly inappropriate under the circumstances, and that things were heating up a notch or three.

"Your... husband," Minerva spat the word at the man opposite her, "just tried to assault me."

"No," Edwina said, though the word was without conviction. Flora got the impression, in fact, that the woman was not surprised by the accusation.

Edwards himself said nothing to deny it. Had said nothing at all since he had been cornered. Certainly not helping his case, though Flora suspected he had no defence to offer anyway. Thankfully, Lily, Shona and Jean had ushered the children away to the craft table up by the farmhouse, which was being run by the Blanchette sisters. Betty had stayed to watch, of course, never one to miss the action.

For a second, everything fell silent, the epitome of the

calm before the storm, until all hell broke loose and Edwina slapped her husband hard across the cheek, at the same moment that Phil – who had been comforting Minerva – also launched at the man. Adam and Laurie had to come between the two, though Phil got in a couple of blows before he could be held back.

"Enough," Stan said resolutely, getting down from the tractor which had just come round after the first trailer ride. Luckily, he had deposited the families at the refreshment barn first, "This is my farm and it's a peaceful place. Doc you need to leave. You're no longer welcome. We respect women here." For a man of few words, Flora thought it was the perfect speech.

"Well, really, perhaps it's a misunderstanding?" Edwina began, now the shock had started to wear off she was no doubt seeing the elevated place the couple had held in village life slipping out from under her.

Minerva looked about to tell the doctor's wife exactly what had happened, so that there could be no misunderstanding, which was something Flora deemed would be better happening in private, "Perhaps, if Pat is here, this could be discussed back at the farmhouse?"

"I'm here, just arrived, sorry had to finish my shift," the local policeman came forward with his trusty sidekick Frank, who was eying Stan's sheepdog Bertie playfully, "ay, I think we should continue whatever this is in private. Let the little'uns have their fun without all the drama."

And with that, Ernest and Edwina, Phil and Minerva accompanied Pat back up to the farmhouse, filing past everyone who had been watching and who now stood gawking in shocked silence.

"Well, let's hope that's all of the unwanted excitement for the day over with," Flora said, as she and Adam walked back to take up their posts at the chocolate station in the main barn.

Oh how little did she know…

NINE

Twenty minutes passed before Minerva and Phil
emerged from the farmhouse, with the Edwards couple
nowhere to be seen.

Good riddance Flora thought, coining one of Reggie's
favourite phrases. She assumed they had left the farm
altogether, since Stan had made it clear the doctor was
no longer welcome. Minerva smiled up at Phil as they
walked past, waving at Flora who was in conversation
with the new schoolteacher, Bunny, and two of the
ladies from the W.I. The teacher herself wore a
homemade costume which involved a black leotard
worn over a long-sleeved top in the same colour and
black shiny leggings. Attached to the leotard were
eight thickly-knitted socks, each stuffed full to make

them stand out at an angle to her body. As far as spiders go, it was… well, rather menacing, given the woman's height and stature. She reminded Flora of Miss Trunchbull from 'Matilda', in fact, with her thick calves and thrower's shoulders and Flora hoped she was nicer to the children in her class than that fictional schoolmistress. Flora made a mental note to be kinder, even in her thoughts – she could only imagine what others must think of her own costume!

"Please Mummy, please, just one more fruit kebab," little Megan dragged on Sally's hand a short while later, pulling her back over to the fondue table, where the fruit covered sticks were lined up and ready to be dipped in the melted chocolate.

"But that'll be your third," Sally said, even though the fight seemed to have gone out of her. Flora thought the vicar's wife seemed tired and frazzled, and decided to do something nice for her in the coming week.

"Me too! And me!" Evie and Charlotte added to the mix, until Flora was taking their mother's money and handing over the treats that the girls were desperate for.

"Thank you," Sally said quietly to Flora when the girls were engrossed in the important business of covering every square inch of fruit in chocolate, "I was hoping to let them run around a bit more, but there seem to be some people that I don't recognise here, so I'm keeping a closer eye."

"Oh?" Flora asked.

"Well, just one man I've seen so far who I don't recall being from either Baker's Rise or Witherham. He seems overdressed for a family event like this too, so…" Sally shrugged her shoulders, "In fact, give me one of those strawberry dippers, Flora, I could do with a sugar hit. It might even help my thumping headache. If you can't beat them, hey?"

"Absolutely," Flora replied, though she was distracted. Although public events like these did sometimes attract visitors, it was seldom the case at this time of year. Theirs was a tightly knit community and, in Flora's experience, strangers turning up didn't bode well. Her stomach churned for a moment as she worried that it might be Gregory, come for her money again, until she remembered he was behind bars for fraud now. Nevertheless, Flora knew she'd feel better if she checked it out.

"Lily," Flora shouted across to where she could see her friend dashing from the small barn which held the barrel of jam, back to the farm shop, "Lily, do you mind if Adam and I take a break?"

"Of course, I'll ask the two Vivs to take over for a few minutes," Lily shouted back.

"Thanks for getting me out of there," Adam said five minutes later as they walked outside, "if I had to serve one more cup of hot chocolate with whipped cream and marshmallows I think I'd have turned into one! I don't know how you do it in the tearoom, one hour on my feet serving and making small talk and I'm shattered!"

"You're welcome, though I did have an ulterior motive."

"Oh?"

Flora shivered as she told Adam what Sally had said, wishing she had thought to bring a cardigan, or even better a coat. The rain was heavier now and they ducked into the jam barn to seek shelter for a moment. Laurie was beside the wooden barrel, a few books of raffle tickets next to him.

"Ah, Flora! Adam! Perfect timing, could you just hold the fort, while I, ah, run to the bathroom?" Laurie asked, red faced, and Flora knew they could hardly refuse.

The barn was empty of customers though, and once

they had marvelled over the sheer quantity of jam that Lily must've produced to fill such a large container – the top of the barrel came up above Flora's waist – the pair sunk down on a rectangular hay bale behind the table that was stacked with jam jars.

"No one will be able to see us, if they come in," Flora whispered with a girly giggle, feeling suddenly like a teenager hiding with her boyfriend.

"Exactly," Adam replied, already peppering kisses from her temple down to her neck.

Their romantic interlude was short-lived, however, as another couple came into the barn. Flora was about to jump up on ticket duty when Adam held her back, "Wait love, something feels off."

Trusting her husband's gut feeling, Flora froze where she was beside him before sinking further back against his side. Sure enough, the pair didn't come forward towards the jam, instead the man dragged the woman to the side of the heavy barn doors, in the dark corner to the left of the entrance.

Flora had the awful feeling they were eavesdropping, yet Adam was right, the atmosphere didn't feel like a lover's tryst or anything innocent, in fact.

"Get off me!" the woman, whose voice Flora immediately recognised as Minerva's, yanked her arm from the man's grasp, "You're the second man this evening who thinks he has a right to touch me. What the hell are you doing here, Rupert?"

"Doesn't a husband have the right to see his wife?"

Flora smothered her gasp. Adam was on his haunches ready to intervene if the man stepped out of line, but for the moment, they stayed put and remained silent.

"Ex-husband!" Minerva ground out.

"Not yet, not quite my love, and then there's the business of the money you owe me," he snarled more than spoke the last bit.

"I owe you?" Minerva's voice rose through her incredulity, "You owe me more like. How much were you siphoning off as my manager? For our future, you said... for your addictions more like. I took what was rightfully mine before I left, and there should've been a lot more of it. What a fool I was to trust you. I have no idea how you found me, but go, Rupert, go and don't come back." For the first time, Minerva sounded worn down by it all.

"Nerva, don't you pull away from me," and that was

Adam's cue. As the man reached to stop Minerva from leaving the barn, Adam jumped up and inserted himself between the two.

"What the..?" Rupert asked.

"Sorry, Minerva, we hadn't intended to overhear," Flora said gently, the sound of her creaking hips filling her ears as she rose to join them.

"It's okay, ah, thank you for saving me… again," Minerva's voice shook, as Adam firmly suggested that Rupert accompany him to the exit.

"Come on, why don't you go to the farmhouse for a quiet cuppa?" Flora linked her arm through the other woman's, "I have to get back to the chocolate stand, but I can ask one of the others to keep you company. Reggie's there, and I know he'd love to see you."

"Actually, Flora, I'm quite tired, do you mind if I just head home? The children's parade was a success, that's the main thing."

"Of course, shall I get Adam to drive you?"

"No thanks, I drove Phil and I up here so I have my car. Perhaps you could give him a lift back home later?"

And with that she left the space, no longer skipping as she had when she arrived, just as the first rumble of thunder rolled loudly overhead.

That'll be the storm finally here, Flora thought, as she hurried to find Lily and suggest they called it day, feeling the electricity in the air. It brought goosebumps to her arms and the heavy rain plastered her hair to her face. It was almost twilight, but the place had suddenly darkened as if it were the dead of night, a combination of the storm overhead and the electricity failing suddenly, plunging them all into inky blackness. Flora had to admit to feeling scared as she ran for the refreshment barn, praying Adam would already be back there.

Bad things can happen in the dark, she knew, and Flora didn't want to be alone when they did.

TEN

Flashlights on phones shone around the cramped sitting room in the farmhouse where Lily was lighting the stock of candles she always kept handy in the sideboard. Farmer Stan was standing at the back door with his big torch, ushering everyone inside, through the kitchen and to join the not-so-merry throng in the main room. Flora cuddled into Adam's side, bouncing little Megan on her knee and stroking the head of the trembling bird on her shoulder, while Sally sat next to her trying to quieten sensitive Charlotte, who quivered and sobbed at the growls of thunder and flashes of lightning. Aaron was entertaining Evie and little Matias with the electronic game he had brought with him while his mum, Shona, helped with the candles.

Betty, Jean and Hilda May sat stoically on the settee opposite with the Blanchette sisters – the former huffing because Jean had cut her off when she began lamenting for the third time about how the weather affected her joints. All in all, they were not a happy group. Not helped, of course, by the fact they were mostly dripping wet, soaked through, and freezing cold.

"Minerva! Minerva! Where is she?" Phil could be heard shouting in from the back door.

"I don't recall seeing her come in, but you'd better check for yerself lad," Stan's gruff voice came through.

Phil appeared in the entrance to the room, his face a ghoulish illumination from the light on his mobile phone, "Minerva!" He repeated loudly, so that all assembled stopped what they were doing and looked at him.

"I haven't seen her, why don't you come in and dry off," Lily tried to calm the man, "Stan, come here and light this fire, would ye? Afore we all freeze to death."

"I think she was planning on leaving after, ah, I saw her in the barn earlier," Flora said, casting a side-eyed glance at her husband, though she knew he wouldn't divulge anything else of the encounter – that was

Minerva's business to tell if she wished.

"Well, the car is still there," Phil snapped back, his once-greased hair now hanging lankly by his ears, and his wizard's cape sitting askew on only one shoulder.

"Really?" Flora's voice held more than a hint of concern now, and Adam moved to his feet beside her.

"I'll help you search," Adam said, "I'll just borrow one of Stan's coats if that's okay, Lily?"

"Aye help yerself, they're on the hook on the back door there."

The vicar also offered, along with Laurie and Will, so it was five men who tramped back out into the wilds of the weather. Pat had already left to go back into the centre of the village, checking the roads and making sure everyone there was doing okay. An ominous silence descended on the women, causing little Charlotte to renew her sobs, as if the atmosphere conveyed a scare factor that couldn't be brushed off with comforting words or more candlelight.

It was a mere five minutes later when Flora received the text from Adam telling her to ask Stan to lock all the doors and to make sure no one left the farmhouse.

She knew then.

She knew that something was terribly wrong, and the little bird on her shoulder picked up on her tension immediately.

"Secrets and Lies! Hide it all! Bad bird!" he screeched, causing Tanya to jump and earning him a swift "Desist silly bird."

Seeing Flora's face, though, her friend knew immediately that something was off, "Flora? What is it?"

"Ah, if everyone could just remain in here until, ah, the roads are cleared, that would be grand," Flora spoke loud enough for all to hear, before quickly adding, "Lily, I believe your stove is gas, so we could boil some pans of water for pots of tea." It was a feeble distraction, but it seemed to work, and gave the women a focus. The children were mostly oblivious, apart from Charlotte who refused to let Sally out of her sight. Tanya, of course, looked completely unconvinced, but was astute enough to not question Flora further.

And so the waiting began.

ELEVEN

"Drowned? In the barrel of jam?" Flora had to swallow down the bile which rose to her throat at the picture in her mind.

"Aye love, had her head submerged until… ah, well, asphyxiated, definitely smacks of foul play, but that's just between you and me. I have to get back out there, Phil's not in a good way, as you can imagine. The roads are flooded down at Baker's Bottom, so neither the police nor the paramedics can get up here. Stan is going down in the tractor to bring Pat back up, so that at least we have one law enforcement officer on the site overnight. Not that it'll do much good – the, ah, damage has already been done."

"But, but, what will I tell everyone?" Flora asked, wishing her lip didn't wobble so dramatically.

"I would suggest you're just honest, to a degree anyway. Are the children in bed?"

"Yes, Lily and Sally got them all settled upstairs shortly after you and the other men left."

"Okay, good, you go in and tell the ladies there's been a murder. I would, ah, leave out the graphic details though, if I were you."

"Oh, absolutely I will," Flora shivered in his embrace, grateful for the knitted shawl Lily had lent her. The matter-of-fact way in which her husband spoke of people being killed, the way he could just flip the professional switch and stay detached, never failed to shock her, no matter how many times Flora was witness to it.

"Has my Stan left yet?" Lily came racing into the kitchen from the hallway, her mobile phone clutched to her chest, more shaken than Flora had ever seen her and she didn't even know about Minerva's demise yet. As far as Lily was concerned, Stan was simply needed to go to the village, seeing as how he was the only one whose vehicle could hopefully make it through.

"No, he's just about to though," Adam replied, "is there a problem?"

"It's Amy, she just called to say she's in active labour and they can't get out of the village. Worse still, the ambulance can't get to them. Both ends of Baker's Rise are flooded now."

"Okay, ah plan of action…" Flora tapped the beak of her feathery companion, her constant source of comfort, as her mind whirred, "you and me Lily, and ah, Shona and Sally we'll pile into the tractor and head back to the village with Stan. That'll be okay, won't it Adam? If there's, ah, no further questions till morning?"

Lily had already rushed off to get the other women, not waiting for Adam's answer and completely oblivious to the drama that had unfolded in her barn.

"Well, we should all stay here really, but seeing as some visitors to the fayre had already left by the time we took shelter, I don't imagine it's necessary for everyone to stay at the scen… ah, at the farm overnight. I'll get Jean and Tanya to help me make a list of everyone who they saw at the event as everyone will need to be interro…ah, found. I'll have to make some calls about that bloke that was with the deceased earlier though. Husband did he say he was? As I imagine he might be hotfooting it out of the area by now. Though the storm could work in our favour, keeping him trapped…" Adam voiced the thoughts running through his head, but Flora had already tuned out, her mind on the new task at hand. If she didn't compartmentalise the horror of another murder into the tiny box in her head reserved for such atrocities, then she would be a gibbering wreck by now.

It was only a matter of minutes before the small group squashed into the cab of the tractor. Thankfully, the bench seat could fit three, and Flora and Sally offered to sit on the floor in the space behind the seat. It was cold, it was cramped and it was dark, but none of them cared. Amy needed her friends, and they were on their way.

Reggie, of course, had had to be prised off Flora's shoulder and made to stay with Betty and Jean, and Flora had no doubt that they wouldn't hear the last of that for a long while yet.

"Stay safe, love," Adam whispered as he shut the door, waved to Stan and the tractor started up.

Flora didn't have a chance to reply, her teeth chattering and grinding with every bump as the old vehicle began to move, the whole machine being buffeted from side to side by the howling wind, despite its size and weight.

They heard Amy before they saw her. Before the front door was even opened in fact, and they were blown in in a flurry of dead leaves and beneath a sheet of rain.

Answering the door, Harry was white as a sheet, with Lewis hanging to his leg, "Quick, please, by the sounds of things there's not much time." He gestured behind him with a quick lift of his eyebrows, clearly not wanting to say more in front of the boy.

"It'll all be fine," Sally said calmly, stepping past the older man and smiling down at Lewis. Harry simply nodded and handed her the torch he had been holding, whilst Flora wished her own demeanour could be even half as peaceful.

"Have any of you delivered a baby before?" Gareth whispered, leaving Amy for a second between her contractions to come to the bedroom door, his voice choked from the scene in the room and his eyes wide at the sight of the women in their fancy dress costumes.

Apparently, Flora thought, *we are a scarier vision than a woman in full-blown labour.* Her own costume was now skin tight and clinging to Flora's skin – another casualty of the deluge they'd endured – so she could only imagine the picture she painted of a middle-aged Lost Boy with all her lumps and bumps on show. *Focus,* she told herself, leaving one of the other women to answer Gareth's very valid question.

"Only our own," Shona replied confidently, striding around to the far side of the bed.

Flora could only follow the others, feeling seriously out of her depth. "Harry?" she said, somewhat confused, before entering the bedroom.

"Aye lass, Gareth phoned looking for my Betty and I was the next best alternative. Just a bit of moral support and a babysitter for Lewis. No idea about the whole delivery thing."

"Well, me neither," Flora admitted, "but needs must…"

By the light of half a dozen candles, and to the playlist she had prepared on her mobile phone, Amy gave birth to a beautiful baby boy with her husband right there beside her. She had done most of the labouring before the team of helpers arrived, and so things seemed to Flora to be moving very quickly. Flora had sent up a double prayer of thanks, firstly for the safe delivery of the child and secondly for the fact that the other women were content for her to be a 'head end only' person, leaving them to work at the main centre of activities, so to speak. The whole delivery was blessed with no complications, and within a couple of hours the new mum was sitting up in bed with a hot cup of sweet tea and two slices of toast and butter, thanks to the electricity coming back on at a very opportune moment! Even Harry wasn't immune from the sudden watery-eye syndrome that seemed to affect them all, and Flora was still sniffing as she answered a call from Adam.

"Is your electricity back too, love?" her husband asked, after enquiring after what he called 'the state of play' with Amy. On this occasion, Flora understood, details were most definitely not required.

"Yes, all good, absolutely beautiful baby boy, but I'm guessing I'll have to go back to the vicarage with the others because you're stuck up at the farm?"

"Yes love, and listen, we don't know who did this up here, or where they may be now, so just watch your back, okay?"

"Will do," Flora snuffled, "get back as soon as you can."

"I will love, I will. Goodnight."

"Goodnight." Despite witnessing the miracle of new life – or maybe because of it – Flora felt the full depth of loneliness which that one word instilled. She left with Harry and the other ladies to spend the night just down the street at the vicarage, closing the door quietly on the beautiful family they had helped, and Flora wasn't sure she had ever felt more bereft.

TWELVE

There was no church service the next day, nothing to wake the sleepy village which looked hardly the worse for wear after the storm that had raged for most of the night. By daybreak, the clouds had cleared, the build-up of water was already dissipating into nearby fields and, save for some misplaced tiles and branches, the image was as serene as any Flora had seen as she looked out of her bedroom window at the vicarage. To be fair, she had barely slept a wink, and morning light was a welcome reprieve from trying to force herself to do so.

As soon as they got back to the vicarage the previous evening, Flora had felt obliged to tell the others about

Minerva. Had she thought it through, though, she would have waited until the morning, as her news understandably had Shona and Sally desperate to get back up to the farm to their respective children. In her desperation and frustration, Sally had railed at Flora for, what she saw as, withholding information that there was a murderer on the loose, and any joy from the new arrival had been replaced with harsh glares and angry silence. Flora hoped that now, in the light of a new day, everything could be ironed out and put to rights.

"Aren't you going to help them with their enquiries?" Flora asked Adam later that day as they cosied up on the sofa of the coach house.

"Nope. Not my job anymore."

Flora scrutinised her husband's expression to see if she could detect any hint of regret in his statement, but found none, "Won't they want to question me? After what we saw in the barn?"

"Absolutely, and me. McArthur has a new partner, ah, a lad called Timpson. Bit wet behind the ears, but he'll learn quickly on the job. They'll have us on their list, don't you worry."

"I'm not, I just want to get the formal stuff out of the way as quickly as possible."

"I know love, I know, but these things need to follow their proper course."

"Of that I'm well aware," Flora said snappishly, before immediately regretting her tone and kissing her husband's cheek by way of apology. He snuggled her closer to his side and they both dozed off.

"Pipe down! Shut yer face!" They were woken by the concurrent sounds of hammering on the front door and screeching from the small bird in the corner, who was in one of the foulest moods Flora had ever seen from her feathery companion. No doubt still in a huff from being left at the farmhouse during the power cut.

"Shut yer beak!" Adam parroted back to him, rising slowly and stretching out his back muscles, "I'm getting far too old to be up all night and then sleeping on the settee."

Flora followed her husband into the hallway and stood back as he invited McArthur and Timpson into their home.

"Wet behind the ears?" Flora whispered as they put on

the kettle and prepared a plate of biscuits, "He looks about twelve! If you hadn't told me beforehand, I'd have thought he was on work experience!"

"Aye well, he is young…" The rest of Adam's words were drowned out by a screech of "Cows loose! Chocks away!" and then a loud guffaw from the younger of the two detectives in the sitting room.

Rushing in, Flora and Adam found McArthur searching for a tissue to remove the rather ghastly little parcel that Reggie has just deposited on her head, whilst she glared at Timpson, who didn't even try to hide the fact he thought it was hilarious.

"Reginald Parrot!" Flora exclaimed, grabbing the remorseless offender and locking him in the bedroom until their company was gone. "I'm so sorry, he's had, ah, an unsettling night."

"Haven't we all," McArthur replied dryly.

"What's that with 'chocks away'?" Adam asked as they hurriedly finished preparing the drinks.

"Too many war films and programmes watched with Harry, I suspect. Whenever Harry helps out with the book shop he likes to borrow my iPad and watch the history stuff that Betty doesn't like him having on the tele at home. Not that there's anything wrong with his choices, just that they don't involve crafts or cooking!"

"Well, I'm sure it's given Reggie some delightful new phrases," Adam replied as they joined their guests.

The detectives took both their statements, including details of the earlier incident between Minerva and Doctor Edwards, and the conversation which they had overheard later between Minerva and her husband. It was a much more relaxed style of questioning than Flora had been used to in the past, and she put this down to the fact that she was with Adam, and his opinion held a lot of weight with McArthur. So much so, in fact, that the detective asked for her former colleague's thoughts on the murder and on likely suspects.

"Well, I'd say finding the husband would be my top priority, then bring the doctor in for a formal interrogation," Adam stopped short, as if he suddenly remembered it was no longer his job.

"And what about the doctor?" McArthur turned her gaze to Flora, who flushed under the sudden scrutiny, "Why could the labouring couple not get Doctor Edwards to help them last night, instead of bringing you women down in the storm?"

"That's a good question," Flora began, wringing her hands, until Adam gently took one and held it in his lap, "Harry, ah Mr. Bentley, that is, told me that Gareth, the new father, had phoned the doctor's house several times, but there was no answer. Harry himself had then hammered on the door, but got the same lack of response."

"Did he say if there were any lights on to indicate they were home?" Timpson chimed in.

"Of course there wouldn't be, it was a blackout," McArthur jumped in to answer him, a sigh of exasperation following her curt words.

"I was just wondering," Timpson bit back, like a scolded child.

Adam raised an eyebrow at the rather unprofessional dynamics between the two but said nothing.

"We've got uniformed officers searching for the husband, but I imagine he's lying low," McArthur said, "we'll get it out in tomorrow's press though, so the public will be on the lookout. Anyway, we've taken up enough of your time."

Flora had the distinct impression that was the detective's polite way of saying that she could no longer hear herself think over the racket coming from the little bird in the bedroom.

Tired, stressed and with a thumping headache, Flora left Adam to show their guests out and headed straight to the bedroom to scold her petulant parrot. No sooner had she turned the door handle, however, than the noise suddenly stopped and a small cooing voice said, "My Flora! So cosy!"

"You're lucky I love you," Flora muttered, letting him jump onto her arm and move in an undainty waddle up to her shoulder.

"Love you," Reggie squawked for the first time ever, causing tears to well in Flora's eyes.

And with those two words, all was forgiven.

THIRTEEN

The tearoom was buzzing the following morning with most of the village women descending on the place to discuss recent events – to share and to support, never to gossip, of course! – with the notable exception of Lily who was understandably still dealing with an invasion of forensics people and police up at the farm. Adam had withdrawn to the bookshop out of the way, and Flora really wished Reggie would join him. She had tried to cajole the sulking bird through to that side, even resorting to outright bribery with his favourite grapes, but the stubborn parrot was having none of it. Instead, he sat on his perch in the corner of the tearoom, unusually facing the wall, and obstinately refusing to turn around. After the arrival of the first couple of customers, Flora saw exactly why this was – as soon as Reggie heard the bell tinkle above the door, his bottom wiggled, his tail feathers shot up, and he screeched either "Cows loose!" or "Chocks away!" before letting loose a stinky parcel into the small gravel-lined tray below which Flora kept positioned ready for little accidents.

"Accidents, Reginald Parrot, not deliberate deployments!" Flora muttered as she scooped up after him for the sixth time. How he was producing it all, she had no idea, making a mental note to ask Will if this was normal. But then, when had Reggie ever been normal?

"So, before we get onto more serious matters, did you like our outfits the other night?" Betty asked, when all were assembled again around two tables that had been pushed together.

"Outfits?" Flora asked, recalling only that Betty, Jean and Hilda May had all been wearing the same kind of knitted hat that looked distinctly like a tea cosy, "Were you, ah, teapots?"

"Teapots!" Betty said, aghast, "No, lass, we were the three witches from 'Macbeth'!"

Tanya opened her mouth to speak, but this was one of

the rare occasions on which she thought better of it and instead simply shook her head at Flora, the hint of a smile at the corner of her mouth.

"Anyway," Betty continued, oblivious to the silent exchange across the table, "it was a darn shame, if you ask me."

"Aye she was so young, must've only been about Flora's age," Jean agreed.

"Aye well, but I was talking about the jam. Waste of a lot of good jam, if you ask me."

"But nobody did, Betty!" Sally exclaimed from her seat next to Rosa, jumping suddenly to her feet, "Excuse me ladies, but I've a bad headache, and things to do at the vicarage, I... sorry."

Flora moved to see their friend out, and to offer some help in any form she could, but Sally had grabbed her coat from the stand and was out the door before Flora could squeeze around the table.

"Well, that's not like Sally," Shona said, "not at all."

"She hasn't been herself lately," Tanya agreed.

"I wonder if she's still angry that I didn't mention about Minerva until we were back at the vicarage? I'll pop round later with some soup," Flora said, "to apologise again and see if Adam and I can help out with anything."

"Aye, I'll join you," Betty said, causing three different voices to reply, "perhaps that's not a good idea."

The table went quiet as second cups of tea were poured for everyone, and Flora served more of the 'carrot cake bites' she had salvaged from the cake that hadn't been suitable to take up to the farm. Flora had chopped off the best bits of her final attempt, smothered them in cream cheese icing and was serving them free with every drink.

"Anyway, as I was saying," Betty continued, slyly feeding the whole piece of cake to little Tina after taking a small bite, scrunching her nose up in distaste, and washing the tiny morsel down with a huge gulp of Earl Grey, "it was a long night."

"It really was," Rosa agreed, "what with the sadness, the fear, the darkness."

"I was meaning that I didn't have my knitting with me, wasted good knitting time I did, but I see your point," Betty nodded in a magnanimous fashion, earning her a groan from Tanya.

"I heard her ex-husband was hanging around," Shona said, being the pub landlady meant she generally heard every bit of gossip that flew around the village, "so I'm guessing he did it."

Flora made no comment, not wanting to divulge information that the police may be using.

"Well, in my experience, women who move in with a man after knowing him for just a couple of weeks are generally running from something," Tanya said quietly. Jean rubbed their friend's shoulder gently.

"Aye, I can only imagine the state Phil's in," Jean added.

"He was in the pub last night, drowning his sorrows and lashing out at anyone and everyone," Shona said, "a sad sight, that's for sure."

"Well, he's never been my favourite person, but I think we should rally round if we can, with some meals and the like, even just a bit of company," Flora suggested and they all agreed.

"Did you see that new copper?" Betty asked, "He was just a bairn! I've got crocheted dishcloths older than him!"

"He is on the young side," Flora agreed, smiling,

knowing that Timpson was going to have to work hard to earn the respect of the villagers since he certainly didn't command it the way his predecessor Blackett had.

"Well, I think I'll be going to see that new babby now," Betty said, finishing her fourth cup of tea.

"Really Betty, are you sure they'll want visitors so soon?" Jean asked diplomatically.

"Visitors? No, of course not. But me, I'm like family," Betty puffed out her chest and tied her plastic rain cap under her chin.

"Perhaps I should come with you," Shona said, "to make sure the visit is a short one."

"Good idea," Jean muttered, to an indistinct grumbling from Betty.

Flora stood and began clearing the table as the women pulled on their winter coats and said their goodbyes.

"Is it safe to come out yet?" Adam asked, poking his head through the open partition.

"Yes, just about," Flora said, waving at her friends from the door, while the little bird on her shoulder chirped happily as if he hadn't just embarrassed her at least half a dozen times.

"Thank goodness. I've done all the dusting in there, and was about to resort to one of Harry's documentaries!"

"Hopefully we'll have a quiet afternoon. I've given Tanya the rest of the day off," Flora couldn't suppress the huge yawn which followed.

"Well, I'll be here as long as you are, I'm not leaving you alone while there's a killer on the loose," Adam said, putting his arm around Flora's shoulders and kissing her forehead, "hopefully they'll have him in custody soon, now that his face is in the local papers."

Flora shuddered, hoping never to come face to face with Minerva's husband ever again.

Life doesn't always give us what we wish for, though.

FOURTEEN

With the nights drawing in, it was almost dusk as Flora and Adam shut up the tearoom for the day. Flora wanted nothing more than to sink into a hot, deep bubble bath with a romance novel and a glass of red wine. What she was actually going to do, however, was to make a large pot of hearty soup back at the coach house, and then divide it up into Tupperware containers to take first to the vicarage, and then the other half to drop off with Amy and Gareth on Cook's Row. It even crossed her mind to make a bit extra for Phil, as he also lived on that street, and so Flora got Adam to work chopping vegetables as soon as they returned home.

"Do you even think the Edwards couple can be on the

parish council with what he did on Saturday night, and the fact they're under suspicion for murder?" Flora asked as she stirred the big pot on the stove, "More than that, even, do you think he can still be the village doctor? I mean, what woman in her right mind would want to be alone with him?"

"All valid questions, love, but I reckon McArthur would be happy just to know the pair's location right now," Adam's forehead crumpled in consternation, and Flora tried to smooth the wrinkles with her spare hand.

"Very true," she agreed, "I mean, he's clearly lecherous and she's a cruel snob most of the time, but murder? I'm not sure either of them is capable of that."

"We don't know what we're capable of until the time comes to put us to the test," her husband said sagely, and Flora decided not to pursue the conversation – far too unsettling what with another murder investigation hanging over Baker's Rise.

"Oh, hello Flora, Adam," Sally's voice was flat and her face pale as she answered the front door to the vicarage in her pyjamas. She was not the cheery, vivacious woman Flora knew – far from it – and Flora's own stomach began to churn at the sight of her friend.

"We've just brought some soup," Flora said, feeling now that it was a bit of a feeble peace offering, "and to apologise again for my mistiming in communicating news of the murder to you the other day."

"Don't worry, the girls were safe with James. I overreacted. Something I seem to be doing a lot lately," Sally sighed and gestured them inside.

"We won't come in, thanks," Adam spoke up, seeing the woman's appearance and given that six o'clock was prime family time, "we just wanted to help out a little bit, maybe take something off your plate."

"Well, your lovely wife here has already done that by offering to fund the church. James has put the proposal to the Bishop, so now it has to be discussed by the powers that be," Sally swayed slightly on her feet, and Adam rested his hand gently under one elbow, as she clutched the doorframe with the other hand.

"Is James home now?" Flora asked, concern etched into her own features and mirrored in her husband's.

"No, he's gone to some committee meeting or other in Witherham. We're fine though. I mean, the girls have the television and I've been lying on the sofa. Can't seem to shake this headache."

"Why don't we come in and heat the soup for you all, then Flora could bath the girls while I do the dishes?" Adam asked on the spur of the moment.

"Yes, it would be absolutely no bother," Flora added, as Adam guided Sally back inside, effectively making the decision for her.

"If you're sure," the vicar's wife could barely walk in a straight line, and Flora shared a concerned look with her husband.

"Absolutely," Flora said, "let's get you into bed where you can rest properly, then we'll see to everything and bring you a tray up."

"You're such a blessing," Sally whispered, tears in her eyes, as Flora helped her up the stairs.

"Well, that was rather worrying," Flora whispered as they walked away from the vicarage two hours later, past the green and turned left onto Cook's Row.

"I wonder if I should speak to James, see if he needs a friend to confide in?" Adam pondered.

"That's a good idea, and I'll speak to Jean, she's always

so wise about things like this. Sally mentioned to me that she saw the doctor and he brushed her off with hormonal changes or some such rot, but I really think it would be worth her going to Alnwick and getting properly checked out."

"Me too, love, me too."

They stopped off at Billy's old cottage first, now rented from the estate by Gareth and Amy, and handed over the tub of soup to a very grateful new father.

"We won't come in," Flora said, though she was itching to do just that, "I'll come back later in the week when you're more settled."

"Thank you both" Gareth said, "and for the baby playmat that arrived in the post, very generous."

"You're very welcome," Adam said, leading a reluctant Flora away. She could almost smell the talcum powder and new baby scent from the doorstep, and it had a heady allure.

"Let's drop this one in at Phil's quickly and get home," Adam said, shivering even in his winter coat, "it feels like it might rain or snow even."

"Absolutely," Flora agreed, not planning to spend a minute longer than necessary with the man. If she could leave the soup on the doorstep and just ring the bell, then she would have, but it seemed rather unneighbourly to do so. Especially given his recent bereavement.

There was no need to ring the doorbell, however, as the door already stood open when Flora and Adam arrived, with the hallway blocked by two wrestling men.

"Oi!" Adam shouted, "What's going on here?"

After a couple of failed attempts at inserting himself between the kerfuffle, Adam managed to separate the pair, and Flora couldn't hold back her gasp of shock. That one of the men was Phil was no surprise, but that the other was Minerva's husband came as quite the bolt out of the blue.

"What are you doing here? The police want a word with you," Adam said, restraining the stranger's arms behind his back with one hand and dialling McArthur on his mobile phone with the other in tried and tested fashion, "Rupert, isn't it? Surname?"

"Strangelove," the man muttered, causing Adam to pause. No doubt wondering if he was being taken for a fool.

"Phil?" Flora enquired as the man in front of her caught his breath. Back to his worn out cords and holey jumper, Phil looked like a broken version of the man she had seen in the pub just a short while ago.

"I got home, from the public house," Phil was slurring his words, "and he was here, looking for her, her, her, my Minerva's things. She's gone, Flora!"

"I know, Phil, I know, let's get you sat down and some water. And coffee. Strong coffee," Flora guided him through to the small sitting room, which, to be honest, looked like a photographic bomb had exploded all over the carpet and coffee table.

"Are these your photos?" Flora asked, seeing a much younger Minerva in a lot of them.

"No, hers, all hers. It's all about her, it always will be," Phil was sobbing now, sinking to his knees amongst images of his lost love in a scene which made Flora feel like joining him in his misery.

Pulling herself together, though, she cleared the man a spot on the sofa, helped him sit on it, and then went through to the kitchen unable to stop herself from listening to the conversation in the hallway between Adam and the man he detained.

"How did you find Minerva here?" Adam's voice was gruff.

"What? Oh, I was looking for her, of course, but I'd never have come to this pitiful backwater. Never been north of Coventry before, in fact. More used to the cities of Europe, far more my vibe," Rupert clocked Adam glaring at him and hurried his answer, "a woman called me. Anonymous tip off you could say. Very timely. Where is my darling wife hiding anyways?"

"Timely indeed," Adam replied, knowing that one word could be construed in a way to implicate the man he now kept pinned against the wall. He deliberately ignored Strangelove's last question, figuring he was either faking ignorance of Minerva's death or truly didn't know – either way, Adam didn't care, he would leave it to McArthur to break the news and deal with the man's reaction. This situation was volatile enough. Not knowing if the man in his hold would suddenly turn violent, Adam knew he would never put Flora at risk.

"So, you broke in?" Adam asked, changing the subject.

"I want what's rightfully mine," Rupert replied, admitting nothing. Clearly this wasn't the first time the man had had to answer questions from the law.

"And what would that be?" Adam continued.

"The money my bitch of a wife stole," the noise of him grinding his teeth was not a pleasant one, and could be heard even from where Flora was standing.

"And you think she'd keep it here? And not in a bank account somewhere?" Adam was clearly not convinced, and neither was Flora.

No. If she was a gambling woman she'd bet there was something else in Phil's house that Minerva's husband was after, something that could perhaps give the detectives a possible motive.

It was a hunch, but Flora hurried back into the sitting room and offered to come around the next day to help Phil sort through Minerva's belongings. Legally, she supposed the late woman's husband would have the most claim to them, so she would have to act quickly if she were to find any evidence before it was removed as, well, evidence. The police had obviously not come looking here yet, given that they were still taking statements from everyone who had attended the Autumn Fayre, searching for the man in the hallway as well as the local doctor and his wife, and going through any forensic evidence left at the actual crime scene, but they wouldn't neglect the deceased's home for long, even if she had really only just moved in.

"I'm not ready to put her into a box in the attic," Phil sobbed.

"And we won't, but you can't live like this," Flora spoke slowly, hoping to get through to his inebriated brain, "at the very least, let's sort everything out so it's not getting ruined underfoot. It looks like you just tipped a few boxes of her belongings out onto the floor here." Phil blushed and Flora knew that was exactly what he had done. She understood, of course, or could at least empathise, but if the dark storm cloud still hanging metaphorically over the village was to be lifted, then Phil couldn't be left to act alone.

"Thank you, Flora," Phil whispered, as his head lolled to the side and he nodded off, clutching to his chest a photo of he and Minerva at the book fair where they met.

Prising the picture gently from his grasp so that it wasn't completely crumpled, Flora peered closely at the image. Then she took her mobile phone from her handbag and snapped a picture of the photograph, returning the original to the pile on the sofa as the familiar sound of sirens filled the air once again.

FIFTEEN

Despite squinting and twisting at odd angles so much that her face could be legitimately entered into a gurning competition, Flora couldn't make out the name of the book on the table in front of Phil and Minerva at the book fair.

"You look!" she thrust her phone at Adam, the photo zoomed to the max.

"It's just a blur," he replied, zooming back out to try to get a clearer image and risking his wife's wrath.

"I know, but I think that might be the key. What if she was writing a salacious tell-all? Something that her ex-manager wouldn't want to go public?"

"Well, I think you might be jumping the gun a little, love…"

"It's a gut feeling, Adam!" Flora added, knowing she sounded petulant.

"Well, you go over to Phil's tomorrow morning, like you promised and I'll watch the shops with Tanya, but if you find anything we turn it straight over to the police. Agreed?" Flora got the distinct impression her husband was humouring her.

"Agreed," Flora muttered as she stomped off to brush her teeth. How annoying it was to live with someone who was the voice of reason to your own sometimes outlandish schemes!

As with all great plans – or those in Baker's Rise, at least – it went decidedly awry. When she saw the vicarage number pop up on her mobile phone following a rude awakening by the same device at five the next morning, Flora knew something was seriously amiss.

"Sally?" Flora tried to speak through the dry, cotton wool-like feeling in her mouth.

"Flora, it's James. The ambulance is here. They need to

take Sally in. Flora, I'm sorry to ask, but can you come round and watch the girls? I have no one else…" The vicar spoke so fast the message was garbled, but the gist was clear and Adam was already dressing when Flora ended the call.

"Bad bird! Bad bird!" Reggie flew around the room, worried by the sudden change in atmosphere and annoyed at having his beauty sleep so rudely interrupted. Flora paused what she was doing to stroke his head feathers and promised they would pick him up as soon as they could. She herself felt unsettled as worry for her friend gnawed at her, but couldn't take any longer to reassure the parrot as the pair rushed from the coach house without even a quick cup of coffee to sustain them.

Taking the car, they were at the vicarage in a matter of minutes, just in time to see the back of the ambulance as it drove away with siren sounding and lights flashing, making only a small dent in the early morning fog.

"I'll follow them in the car," James said, handing Flora a heavy keychain which looked like it had the wherewithal to open every door in the vicarage, church and hall. He didn't explain further, though his ashen face said everything. After an uncharacteristic hug, the vicar hurried off around the side of the building to the garage, leaving Flora and Adam on the doorstep.

"I'll make us a brew," Adam said, his hand resting gently on Flora's lower back as she walked into the house first and he made sure to lock the door behind them.

"Let's let the girls slee…"

"Mummy?" Little Megan was waddling down the main staircase in a penguin onesie, her hair sticking out and a ragdoll squashed under her armpit.

"No love, it's Flora and Adam."

"Miss Flora? You want your hair and nails done again?"

"Ah, maybe, yes, maybe, once we've had breakfast. But we have to be quiet so as not to wake your sisters, it's still night-tim…"

"Miss Flora!" Evie charged down the stairs with quiet Charlotte following slowly behind, rubbing her eyes and holding her cuddly rabbit by one pink ear.

"Ah, so, breakfast and maybe some calm stories, at least until the sun comes up," Flora yawned, "and let's play a game where we all just whisper…"

The grandfather clock in the study at the vicarage had barely chimed nine o'clock when a small group of women had formed at the front door, eager to hear why there was an ambulance leaving the house in the early hours. Led by Betty and Hilda May, the concerned women of the W.I. had only the best interests of the vicar's family at heart, of course. They certainly weren't desperate to be the first to hear any hot gossip.

"I'm afraid I have nothing to tell you," Adam said firmly, as if he were being interviewed by the press in a professional capacity, "nothing to comment at this time."

"Come on lad, you must know something," Betty piped up, one arm clutching little Tina to her chest, the other resting on her ample hip, "the vicar's wife has certainly seemed peaky lately."

"I'm sure if and when there is anything to report, the vicar himself will be in touch," Adam said, smiling and closing the door on any further retort.

"Those ladies can be a force to be reckoned with, I'm not sure they'll give up easily," Flora whispered when Adam returned to the dining room, where the girls were eating their second breakfast.

"I'm used to questions that I have no intention of answering, don't you worry, love," Adam winked once and helped himself to another bowl of Cheerios. Flora, however, could barely stomach her coffee let alone any food. Her heart was in her mouth with worry for her friend.

"Gonna see your birdie?" Megan asked, milk dribbling down her dimpled chin.

"Yes, yes, we'll get you all dressed and then go and collect Reggie from the coach house. Then we'll visit Miss Tanya in the tearoom, where you can choose a book each from the library shelf in the bookshop and we'll have hot chocolates. Then we'll maybe head up to the big house to read the new stories. Perhaps even play a game of hide and seek up there, it has lots of rooms, you know," Flora found herself waffling, making up an itinerary on the spot which she hoped would keep the children distracted for long enough that they didn't ask about their parents.

For a few hours, at least.

SIXTEEN

The tearoom was of course buzzing with excited anticipation, the villagers attracted like moths to a flame at the prospect of something new to discuss. Sadly, poor Minerva's death was already yesterday's news.

"I'm not sure we should take them in there," Flora whispered to Adam, her teeth chattering in the chilly air as the girls chased Reggie up and down the gravel driveway.

"Well, you have more right than anyone to be there, you don't need to say anything. After all, what do we really know?"

"True, true. Come on girls, let's get a hot drink to warm us up."

"Welcome to the tearoom!" Reggie squawked proprietorially as he led the girls inside, where all conversation immediately stopped and every eye was on them.

"M-M-Miss Flora?" Charlotte asked, her bottom lip quivering.

"Nothing to worry about, sweetheart," Flora rubbed the back of the girl who was clinging to her side, "we're going into the bookshop, remember? We'll have the hot chocolates in there today."

The anxious girl let Adam take her with her sisters to look at the books, whilst Flora faced the inquisition from her neighbours. She took a steadying breath filled with the familiar aroma of coffee and home baking. It was both calming and reassuring. Like a warm hug, it was home.

"Is she dead?" Vivienne Blanchette was the first to speak up, rudely asking what Flora hoped wasn't the first thing on everyone else's mind.

"Who? Sally?" Flora replied curtly, "Why would you ask such a thing?"

"Just ignore her," Genevieve cut in.

Taking the advice and ignoring them both as well as the whispering from each table she passed, Flora walked up to the counter. She was about to speak privately to Tanya, whom she had messaged earlier that morning with only the briefest of details, but then something snapped in Flora and she turned to face the people she was normally thankful to call friends. Jean was absent, working in the local shop as usual, as were Shona and Lily, so it was mainly the esteemed ladies of the Women's Institute who sat poised for information.

"Ladies, I understand in a quiet place like Baker's Rise, everyone knows each other's business. Not only that, but they see it as their right to have that information. Believe me, that is neither healthy nor helpful for anyone. Yes, there was an ambulance at the vicarage, yes the vicar's wife was taken ill, no we don't know anything further. To speculate would be unkind to the family we love as one of our own. Those girls through there need your support, need you to make things normal for them, and need you to act like compassionate adults and not gossip-crazed country bumpkins."

Flora took several deep breaths, but didn't break eye contact with the women seated in front of her, who mostly sat with open mouths and wide eyes.

"Well, I… of course no one wants to upset the girls. We only want to know what we can do for the family," Betty spoke up, looking suitably abashed.

"I know, I know," Flora softened her tone and smiled at her friend, "and the best thing you can do right now, is to go about your day and talk about something else. You ladies are the backbone of this village, couldn't you put your energies into something that would benefit the whole of Baker's Rise? Maybe the talent show? Now that George and Pepper Jones have moved to Scotland to be with their daughter, we'll be without her usual organising – we'll need to start working on that this month. Or the Christmas decorations for the village green, you ladies always make the place look beautiful. Didn't you win an award one year?"

"Yes, nineteen eighty-three," Hilda May replied proudly, "I was given special recognition for a Christmas pudding post-box cover I knitted."

"Excellent, well, why don't I get you ladies another few pots of tea and some scones on the house and you can put your thinking caps on," Flora gave a satisfied nod to Tanya and the two began preparing the drinks as a newly industrious buzz filled the place.

There had been story time on the cosy sofa in the study, hide and seek in the upstairs bedrooms, musical statues in the empty function room and finally a brisk hop, skip and jump around the gardens. Flora, Adam and Reggie were shattered. The girls, not so much.

"Where do they get all the energy? And without caffeine?" Adam asked, as Flora pretended to be judging a jumping competition between the puddles which still remained after the storm.

"I have no idea. If you could bottle it, we'd make a fortune," Flora spoke around her yawn, "let's head back to lock up the big house and go back to the vicarage. We could put a film on for them."

"I like your thinking," Adam agreed, as Evie challenged him to a race back to the front door.

Flora, Charlotte and Reggie travelled at a much more sedate pace, as they watched little Megan try to keep up with her big sister. Rounding the final corner between the hedges, they almost bumped into the tall woman who strode up the driveway towards the main doors.

"Genevieve," Flora couldn't muster up any enthusiasm in her greeting for a woman she had only ever crossed swords with during their brief acquaintance.

"Flora, I ah, I was wondering if I could have a quick word? Tanya said she thought you had headed up here earlier."

"Charlotte, can you run on ahead and tell Adam I'll just be a couple of minutes?" Flora asked.

The girl didn't look too sure, until Reggie jumped from Flora's shoulder to her much smaller arm. Having a little feathered companion seemed to embolden her, and Charlotte skipped off happily, with Flora watching her into the building.

Finding a spot on a thankfully dry stone bench, Flora tapped the spot next to her.

"So, Genevieve…"

"Please, call me Genie. I prefer it, my late father's nickname for me."

"So, Genie, what can I do for you?" Flora's tone was all business.

"Well, of course I want to apologise for my sister's comment earlier. She has few social skills and tact isn't among them. Our mother liked to keep us both close to her and together with each other, so we have led a more sheltered life than most."

"I understand. Hopefully Vivienne will learn those skills quickly, or else keep her thoughts to herself, otherwise she will hurt and alienate those she wishes to befriend," Flora replied, thinking a moment later that she had spoken too harshly but not apologising for it. Hard truths were hard to hear, she knew.

"I agree," Genie twiddled with the frayed hem of her scarf, "it's actually the other thing I want to talk to you about, Flora. I, ah, I know we got off on the wrong foot with the misunderstanding about the tearoom…"

Flora didn't think there had been any misunderstanding at all. As far as she was concerned, conflict had arisen from the sisters' presumption. Wanting to keep the conversation quick, though, she bit her tongue on her thoughts on the matter. These had been shared very vociferously at the time and wouldn't be any easier for the repetition.

"But, ah," Genie continued, "I was wondering if you might need a housekeeper here, at The Rise?"

Of all the things Flora might have expected the woman to say, that was not one of them. She had promised the two sisters the opportunity to organise a themed evening in aid of charity in the new year, but had never once mentioned any permanent vacancy.

"Well, I'm not sure about staffing for the place at the moment," Flora spoke the truth, "this year has been a bit of a whirlwind… or, rather, a rollercoaster. I will think about it though, however even if I were to need someone there would only be the one position available."

"And, erm, would lodging up here be included?" Flora studied the woman opposite her intently, and saw only sincerity in her features. There was no game playing or levity as Genie spoke again, "I wish to make a fresh start, even at my time of life, and I thought maybe you would understand something about that. I wish to break away from my sister, to live independently and pursue my own goals. Without any funds other than those tied up in our family home, however…"

"I do understand, yes," Flora softened her tone, "and if I find myself in need of a housekeeper, you will be first on my list to interview. As regards board, well I had my fingers burned on that front a while ago, when I gave a room to a certain gardener… ended very badly, very badly indeed… but, ah, I will give some thought to it, yes."

"Thank you, Flora, thank you," the woman stood, her camel wool coat hanging limply on her shoulders as if it was meant for a person much broader.

"You're welcome," Flora stood swiftly and hurried back to find Adam. She could feel the vibration of an incoming text message on the phone in her pocket and was almost dreading what it would say.

The message had been from Phil and not James, panicking that the police were there, going through Minerva's belongings and bagging up anything they thought might be useful to their investigation. Flora had already let him know she couldn't come around as planned, but sent a quick reply saying she would still visit as soon as she could.

"McArthur will be wanting to take him to the station today anyway, for a full statement on how he knew Minerva, how long for and so on," Adam said, "best to keep out of it."

"Hmm," Flora replied, thinking suddenly how quiet the house was. If there was one thing she did know about children despite not having her own, it was that silence was never a good sign. Rushing through to the study, however, they found all three girls snuggled up and asleep on the couch, a little green bird nestled between then and snoring loudly.

Such a peaceful sight and, as Flora was about to learn, unfortunately the calm before the storm once again.

SEVENTEEN

It was teatime when the vicar phoned Flora at the vicarage to check on the girls and to tell her that he would be home later that evening. He didn't share many details, sounding too choked up to do so, Flora thought, other than to say that Sally had had some scans and needed a big operation the next day. He would leave her overnight to come home to the children, but would need to be back at the hospital first thing in the morning. Of course, Flora had offered to stay at the vicarage overnight, to save him the journeying back and forth, but James simply stated that Sally wanted him to be the one to explain to their girls what was happening, and Flora understood.

"All okay?" Adam asked, standing at the Aga in the large vicarage kitchen where he had a big pan of boiling water ready to cook pasta for them all. He had a cuddly bunny stuffed into the front pocket of the apron he wore and a fetching necklace of bright, plastic beads around his neck.

At any other time, Flora would have joked about the cute sight he made. Right now, though, she simply tried to force words past the huge lump in her throat, "No, not at all. I think it's something serious. Sally has to have an…"

"What does Mummy have to have?" Evie asked, appearing in the doorway. Little ears, always listening.

"Some more time in the hospital," Adam said quickly, "which is great for me, because you'll have time to paint my nails!"

"Ooh!" the girl squealed, "I'll go and choose a colour. Or, how about, rainbow hands?"

"Sounds perfect," Flora could almost hear the groan in her husband's voice, but the little girl who had already charged off up the stairs was oblivious. She walked over and wrapped her arms around his waist, laying her head against Adam's chest.

"Thank you," she whispered.

When the vicar arrived home past nine o'clock, he found three little girls fed, bathed and tucked up in bed, a grumpy parrot desperate for his home perch, and two adults who felt like they'd been run over by a steam roller.

"I can't tell you how grateful I am," James gave them a watery smile.

"We'll be back first thing tomorrow to look after them for as long as you need," Flora said gently.

"Well, ah, Sally's parents should be arriving tomorrow evening, so, ah they can take over then," the man scrubbed a tired hand through his hair and Flora didn't ask for any more details, knowing he would share when he was ready, "no doubt there's been talk?"

"Well, it's inevitable, but we won't be feeding it," Flora reassured as she put on her coat.

"It's going to be a long road," James whispered.

"With you every step of the way, my friend," Adam shook the vicar's hand, then pulled him in for a hug, before surreptitiously wiping his own eyes and heading off into the dark with his wife.

The next day seemed to dawn very quickly. For once, Flora had slept like a log, yet she woke to their alarm feeling groggy and unrested. They left a very disgruntled parrot in the coach house and took the car to the vicarage, as the leaves which had just a week ago seemed beautiful in their tans and russets, were now nothing more than a wet mulch which was very slippery underfoot.

It took a long while for the vicar to open the heavy wooden door and when he did it was to reveal three wailing girls, who each clung to a different limb making him look like a very unhappy tree.

"Oh!" Flora exclaimed before she could catch herself.

James' eyes were red rimmed and swollen, he wore the same clothes as the previous day and clearly had not slept.

"Let us distract them while you have a quick shower," Flora encouraged in a whisper.

"No!" Charlotte squealed as Flora tried to gently prise the girl off her father.

For once, Evie didn't even acknowledge the visitors' presence, seeming keen to continue the conversation which must have been taking place before her father managed to answer the door.

"I heard you, Daddy, I heard you, talking to the Big Boss last night. You were sad, Daddy, and shouting," she pointed to the ceiling as a general indication of Heaven and Flora had to turn away to hide the sudden swell of tears in her eyes.

"Ah, yes, yes, sometimes we need to ask God some, ah, personal questions," James knelt beside the eldest of his daughters, whilst Adam shut the door with little Megan in his arms. Flora held Charlotte to her and buried her face in the girl's apple-smelling hair.

"And does he answer?" Evie asked, ever the astute one.

"Sometimes, sometimes," James replied, making eye contact with his daughter, "but not always in the time or the way that we want."

"If I ask, will he bring Mummy home?" Evie continued, unperturbed by the tears now streaming down her father's cheeks.

"You should always ask Him, sweetie," the man

choked out, resting a shaking hand on his daughter's head. He motioned for the other two as well and they ran to him, covering his lap as all four sat on the floor. Flora wanted to move, to give them some privacy, but her feet were rooted to the floor. Adam put his arm around her shoulders and they both bowed their heads in shared emotion.

"Listen girls," James began, "Mummy has a Mr. Grumpy in her head, and the doctors need to do an operation to get him out. He's so cosy living there, that it might take Mummy a while to feel better."

"He's a Mister Silly!" Little Megan chuckled, still too young at four to understand the implications of her father's words.

Flora clasped her hands over her mouth to silence the sob which was trying to escape.

"But he will leave? And Mummy will be okay?" Evie asked, sucking her lower lip in consternation.

"Let's keep asking the Big Boss for that," James said shakily, pointing to the ceiling in a moving repetition of his daughter's earlier action.

Showered and changed, the vicar left twenty minutes

later. A shadow of a man who slipped out of the back door silently so that his daughters wouldn't notice.

EIGHTEEN

Flora had been too tired to attend Jazzercise on Wednesday evening, having looked after the Marshall girls until their grandparents arrived at the vicarage at seven in the evening. When Thursday dawned wet and dark, with more of a feel of winter than of autumn, Flora was inclined to snuggle back down in bed and forget about her responsibilities. She could hear Adam whistling to himself in the kitchen, though, making breakfast for them both – years of enforced early mornings and necessary timekeeping hard to shift – so she dragged herself through to that room to join him.

"My Flora!" Reggie chirped from his position on the kitchen counter, where he had clearly just finished scoffing a huge grape. Bits of green skin were still attached to his beak, and the little bird was looking distinctly pleased with himself.

"You look a bit worn out, love, do you want me to hold the fort with Tanya?"

"No, thanks, it's tempting, but I need to put in an order for festive children's books and bake some more scones and muffins. Then after the lunchtime rush I need to pop round to check on Phil as I promised. Life goes on, eh?"

"It does, love, it does."

And they both tried hard not to think about Sally, James and the girls.

Flora sat on Phil's ancient settee later that day, trying hard to stay alert and interested. She had huge sympathy for the man, of course, given that he had just lost the woman he believed to be his soulmate, but half an hour had gone by with nothing but his lamentations, and Flora had to admit her well of compassion was running dry.

"I just loved her so much, you see," Phil carried on, oblivious, "had even asked her to elope with me."

Flora's ears perked up at that, knowing as she did that Minerva still had a husband, "And what did she say?"

"Ah, well, it was very sudden of course, I think I surprised her with my er, romantic side, so she said she needed a little while to think about it."

"Hmm," Flora replied, "and do you remember the man you were tussling with the other day?"

"Vaguely, er, sorry about that, Flora, was a bit deep in my cups at the time."

"I noticed, Phil, I was just wondering if you know who the man was who had broken in here?"

"He told me who he was. I didn't want to believe it. I mean, I'm sure my Minnie would've told me in her own time, she just obviously didn't want to give that bast... that git any more head space."

"Umhm, I understand," Flora nodded, thinking that perhaps Minerva had had her own reasons for not telling Phil the whole truth. Reasons such as a place to hide while she looked for a publisher for her book... *On that note*, "Er, Phil, while I'm thinking about it, I've been considering getting a stand at the next local book fair and I was wondering what your advice would be? Did Minerva have many books to sell? How did she get on?"

"Oh! Well, um, she had actually just printed a few copies of her manuscript at a local press, the book wasn't published anywhere for people to actually buy yet, she was simply in Carlisle hoping to attract a publisher. Instead she attracted an adult literature writer who gave her his heart…" and he was off again on his loop.

Flora made noises of acknowledgment and understanding, letting the man get it off his chest, while she stood and scanned his bookshelves. Skimming over the salacious content, which she knew to be Phil's own works, she spotted three copies of what looked like a less-than-professional product.

Aha! Flora thought to herself, *Bingo!*

"Is this Minerva's book?" she asked, while Phil paused to wipe his eyes.

"What? Oh, yes, bless her, it's her life's work there in those pages."

"Mind if I take a look?"

"Really? Well, if you're interested…"

"I am," Flora took one of the copies from the shelf and

examined the front cover which read, 'Brrrlesque, Left Out in The Cold: An Exposé of the Industry.'

That'll do it! Flora thought as she took a seat again and flicked through the pages, seeing photos of Minerva with her husband in a chapter entitled, 'Frigid: Betrayal on a Professional and Personal Level.' A frisson of excitement ran through Flora as she asked Phil if she could borrow this copy. Blissfully unaware that she believed it to be the key to his partner's murder, Phil agreed gratefully, happy that Minerva could live on in her writing.

"The police mustn't have spotted the books on the shelf," he said, "they just went through her boxes that were piled up in the spare bedroom and her personal stuff in our room. Didn't seem bothered to take her scrapbooks from her time in the business either though, but they were in my wardrobe and the blokes were hurrying so…"

"Scrapbooks?" Flora asked, innocently.

"I'll get them," Phil scuttled off and returned with four thick, large albums, held together with string, the edges of photographs and event programmes sticking out all around.

"Wow, that's quite a collection," Flora sighed, "and I'd

love to go through them all, but perhaps only the first today? I've got to get back to the tearoom," Flora feigned checking her watch reluctantly. In truth she wanted to get on the phone to Adam and McArthur with her finding. No doubt the police might find more evidence contained within these bursting-at-the-seams tomes though, so Flora carefully untied the string on the first, flicking through the pages of Minerva's earliest days in the acting business before she became a burlesque beauty. She paused to look through a couple of programmes, showing Minerva as the star of the show. Local affairs down south, nothing too big, but no doubt useful steps on her career path.

"Wasn't she beautiful? Always in the limelight, never one to fade into the shadows," Phil gushed.

"Absolutely," Flora agreed, handing back the heavy collection, "let me know if you need anything else Phil. I'm sure the police will be, ah, on top of things."

"Can you believe they tried to implicate me?" Phil asked as Flora put on her coat to leave, "said I lost my rag after Edwards assaulted her. Crime of passion or some such cra… rubbish."

"Well, I know from my own experience they have to investigate every angle," Flora said sombrely.

"True, true," Phil saw her to the door, and Flora breathed in the fresh, country air eagerly. The small cottage had clearly not seen a mop or a duster since long before Minerva moved in, and the thick, stale air was cloying to the senses.

She had her phone in her hand long before reaching the corner of the street, phoning her husband with the tell-all book clutched under her arm.

"So, is that it then, the case closed? All cut and dried?" Flora asked Adam when he came off the phone to McArthur back in the tearoom some twenty minutes later.

"Not quite love, not quite. It's useful evidence, and gives Strangelove an even stronger motive, so they'll bring him back in. He'll be under more pressure this time, McArthur will make sure of it, so hopefully they'll get a confession."

"But they've got their man? We can forget about it all now?"

"It was never your case to solve, love. But yes, I think the murderer has been found. The village can sleep safe again."

"Well, apart from wondering where the dear doctor and his wife are," Flora replied sarcastically, "I can't imagine they'll stay away for too long, their possessions are all still there at their cottage."

"And how do you know that?"

"Betty tripped on some leaves the other day and landed close to their front window," Flora raised her eyebrows and Adam shook his head, though his smile conveyed humour at their friend's antics.

"Well, I'm not sure what we can do even if they do return," Adam said, "the villagers can't simply set up a vendetta against them, even if he is a snobbish letch."

"Hmm," Flora said thoughtfully, "we'll see."

NINETEEN

Flora was still working in the book shop at half past six that evening, trying to sort out her seasonal inventory and deciding whether to add some gifts and homeware to her festive offering – knowing she had left it all far too late – when the women from the Knit and Natter group started to arrive. Sally was normally in charge of setting up the chairs in a circle and making the drinks as Flora herself didn't normally attend, so Flora had already begun this, a heavy sadness enveloping her. She had asked James what she should tell the group, and he had asked that she just be honest. There was no point in hiding the truth when it would all come out anyway, and the facts were better than the ridiculous rumours that had already started circulating around the village, that the vicar's wife had given birth to triplets, and that her husband was not the father. *Seriously,* Flora wondered, *do they compete to see who can come up with the most far-fetched scenario?*

"Welcome to the tearoom," Reggie squawked happily from Flora's shoulder as Betty, Jean and Hilda bustled in out of the cold, "so cosy!"

"Aye it had better be," Betty answered him, "I'm chilled to the bone."

"The kettle's on, Betty, and there's fresh scones with jam," Flora assured her friend, receiving a grateful smile in reply.

Rosa arrived next, followed by Bunny and Tanya who appeared to have struck up a conversation on the way there.

"Did you know Bunny used to be actress like me?" Tanya asked, shrugging out of her zebra-print raincoat to reveal an almost ankle-length knitted dress, in rainbow stripes which jarred against each other – a veritable 'coat of many colours' which held Flora transfixed for a moment.

"Pardon? Oh, no I didn't, that's nice," Flora replied from where she stood now behind the counter, preparing the tray with cups and saucers.

"Yes, and I've roped her into helping with the talent show," Tanya said excitedly.

"Oh, that is good news," Flora replied, handing Tanya the tray and turning to fill the two large teapots that were waiting on the counter.

When all the women, about twelve in total, were happily ensconced on the circle of chairs in the bookshop, Flora took a spare seat and explained in as few words as possible – so as not to become too emotional and unable to finish – that Sally had just undergone brain surgery, and that chemo- and radiotherapy would follow. There were shocked gasps, and many tears shed as the group shared how much the vicar's wife had brought to village life in the year the family had been in Baker's Rise.

"I'm sure, in due course, the family will be grateful for meals and help around the home, but for now I'd suggest we give them some privacy," Flora concluded the discussion, "and of course let's not discuss their situation beyond this."

Everyone nodded their agreement, even Betty who had never hidden the fact that she loved the Marshall family, and a heavy silence fell on the room, just as there was a hammering on the door.

"Get out of it! Stupid jerk!" Reggie shrieked, having just fallen asleep with a full tummy.

"It's just me," Lily's voice penetrated the glass and Flora hurried to let her in, "sorry I'm late, it's been manic up at the farm. What've I missed?"

Flora and the ladies gave a brief update on Sally and then all eyes remained on the farmer's wife.

"So, tell us, what's the verdict? What have the police said about the murder?" Betty asked, her old eyes shining.

"Well, we've had the whole barn area roped off for days, there was no access to the farm at all for the first forty-eight hours other than for authorised police and the like. They put their white tents up, and then what with all the comings and goings, churning up the mud and setting the animals off. And the questions, so many questions, it's near sent my Stan mad. He's a man of simple pleasures, likes his peace and quiet you know, and for that to be shattered into pieces, well, he's not a happy man, I can tell you. I've had to make his favourite meals on repeat to soothe him, and there's only so much tripe a woman can eat..." she patted her stomach looking slightly green around the gills, "Have they spoken to you all too?"

The resounding answer was that yes, everyone had given an informal statement. Flora didn't expand on anything she knew about the case, and simply listened as the ladies hypothesised about who the murderer might be and what could have provoked them to commit such an awful act.

"My money's on Doctor Edwards," Tanya said flatly, in a tone that brooked no argument, "horrible man, mauling poor Minerva like that. And last time I went to see him about a rash he told me to stop wasting his time!"

"Yes, he didn't want to hear about my ear infection either," Jean agreed, "I almost had a burst eardrum by the time I went to the walk-in centre in Alnwick."

Flora was shocked as almost every woman in the room had a personal anecdote which contributed to the evidence that Ernest Edwards was not the GP the villagers needed.

"They're back you know," Betty said, looking smug to have this particular titbit to impart.

"Who? The Edwards?" Tanya asked, incredulous, "I didn't think he'd dare show his face around here again!"

"Well, I'm guessing they have nowhere else to go, not indefinitely," Jean surmised.

"Well, they're not welcome," Lily said, with more vehemence in her voice than Flora was used to hearing from her friend.

There was another chorus of agreement, punctuated by the clacking of knitting needles, and Flora decided to change the subject before the ladies actually began planning something, "Rosa, you crochet so quickly and so smoothly, I'm envious of your talent."

"Oh, thank you, it is all in the muscle memory, and the fact that I have been doing it since I was a girl..." Rosa began, only to be interrupted by Betty.

"Ooh! That reminds me! You know that television programme that I like, 'Yarn Wars'? Well, they film at a different location each time, and I've applied for them to come to Baker's Rise for one of the episodes in the next series!"

Everyone looked at her wide-eyed and open-mouthed for a moment. Poor Hilda May dropped her ball of wool and it landed in her teacup which she'd placed on the floor next to her chair, prompting little Tina to jump on it as if it were a toy sent from above.

Concerned by the sudden silence, Reggie tried to fill the void, "What a corker! We're a team!" he squawked, attempting to lighten the mood.

The thought of a full TV crew, all the contestants and paraphernalia, filled Flora with horror. Despite the fact it might mean extra income for the tearoom, the pub and so on, the cost, in her opinion, was too great.

"Betty, I'm not sure that's such a great idea," Jean said what they were all thinking, "did you run it by the parish council?"

"Council shmouncil," Betty clacked her teeth together, "the village needs new things on the horizon. Anyway we probably won't get chosen, little place like this."

"I hope not," Lily said firmly, and Flora nodded, "and you really should run things past the council in future. I know that a lad from Witherham applied to open a takeaway in the empty Jones bakery, 'Baker's Rise Burgers and Fries,' I think it was to be. Anyway, he was given a resounding no."

"Quite right too," Betty agreed, "we need any new businesses to be in keeping with the traditional tone of the village."

Totally oblivious to the self-contradiction, Flora thought, though she didn't pick Betty up on it.

There were much more important developments in village life to dwell on at the moment, so Flora let her mind drift to those instead as the chatter continued around her. The little bird on her shoulder chirped gently beside her ear, and Flora tried to settle the anxious churning of her stomach. If village life was to return to its untroubled state, Flora decided that she, as 'Lady of the Manor' would step up and make sure that it happened.

Regardless of who she might offend in the process.

TWENTY

"Oh, he is gorgeous," Flora exclaimed, beaming down at the baby cradled in her arms, a little curl of blond hair peeking out from under his tiny hat, "how are you feeling, Amy?"

"Tired, happy, did I mention tired? Gareth thought a bit of fresh air and a trip out would be good for me and little Barney here."

"Barney! Oh, it suits him! Doesn't it suit him, Flora?" Tanya gushed.

"It certainly does," Flora agreed, as she watched her husband make his silent escape through to the bookshop. The little parrot sulking in the corner had not taken his beady eyes off the bundle in her arms, and Flora thought how apt the colour green was on him at that moment. Not caring that his beak had been put out by her fussing over another, Flora rocked the baby boy and joined in with Tanya's coos and aahs.

Within seconds, however, the seemingly calm child had morphed into a screaming, red-faced bundle, and Flora quickly handed him back to his mother.

"Is it okay if I breastfeed in here?" Amy asked, blushing.

"Absolutely, you go for it," Flora replied, going to fetch the new mother a glass of juice and a ginger biscuit.

Five minutes later the bell above the door tinkled, and Reggie let out the full force of his disgruntlement on the newcomer, "Get out of it! There'll be hell to pay! Bad Bird! Cows loose!"

"Be quiet, silly bird," McArthur, completely unfazed by the tirade, came into the tearoom followed by Timpson, who stood, frozen to the spot in the doorway as soon as his eyes clocked Amy feeding her baby at the table nearest the door.

"Oh, er, excuse me, I mean, I don't, ah, oh dear," and

with those words of little sense, he turned on his heel and left again.

"He's such a child," McArthur grumbled, "about as useful as a chocolate teapot. Is Bramble around?"

"Yes, yes, I think he's just pottering around the bookshop. I'm sure he'll be glad of the company," Flora said, though she got the distinct impression this was not a social visit.

"So?" Flora asked her husband a couple of hours later, when both shops were empty and Tanya had finished for the day, "What did McArthur want?"

"Oh, just the benefit of my wisdom and clarity," Adam winked at her and Flora couldn't help but smile back.

"On the subject of..?" she pressed.

"There was forensic evidence at the scene of the murder that they can't tie to Rupert Strangelove. It's the only thing between them and the arrest, unless they can get him to confess first." Adam knew that he no longer had to ask his wife to keep information like this to herself, it went without saying.

"What kind of evidence? Like DNA or something?"

Flora only knew what she'd seen on detective shows and read in books.

"Sadly not that cut and dried, I'm afraid. No, it was some silk strands or something – definitely man-made fibres. Caught on the back zip of the deceased's outfit. Only a tiny amount, from clothing McArthur thinks, when the murderer bent over Minerva's back to hold her dow... anyway, shall we have a cuppa while it's quiet?"

"Hmm, and they don't think it came from Strangelove?" Flora wasn't distracted so easily.

"It may have done, but may have doesn't get a conviction, love."

"What colour was it?" Flora asked, her curiosity piqued.

"White, I think McArthur said, but best we leave it to her, eh?"

"Yes, yes, of course," Flora replied, but her brain had already started whirring.

"Don't think I can't see that your brain's just gone into overdrive," Adam joked, kissing Flora passionately. That certainly was more of a distraction than the offer of a hot drink, but still she couldn't stop her mind from going back to the night of the Autumn Fayre, and the costumes that everyone was wearing.

"Edwina was all in white," Flora blurted out, the moment the kiss had ended, "and Betty said last night that the couple are back in the village. Perhaps the doctor and his wife worked together to finish Minerva off. They certainly had motive enough after that scene earlier in the evening. Neither were happy that Minerva had spoken up about Ernest's actions. Maybe they were worried she'd press charges."

"Hmm," her husband paused, "actually, I think I'll just call McArthur. Also, I wasn't going to mention it to you, love, but she did say that they'd been round to the Edwards' house last night after a tip off from one of the villagers that they were back – I think we can guess who – and that the doctor's wife was throwing around accusations about you and Minerva having set up the whole incident to disgrace her husband and raise your own profile in the village. I think I'd like a word with that particular couple myself."

"What? Why of all the nerve! But please Adam just follow your own advice and leave it to the professionals."

"This isn't about the case love, it's about her badmouthing my wife. Which I won't allow. Anyway,

I'll call McArthur with the fancy dress info and then we'd better start clearing up. What time has James called the special parish council meeting for?"

"Five o'clock," Flora said sadly, "I think I have a feeling what he's going to say."

Flora had a strange sense of déjà vu as once again she found herself sitting around the table in the vicar's study with the other members of the parish council. The only difference being that now it was Adam sitting at the desk ready to take the minutes and not Sally. James had just finished giving them all a brief update on his wife, saying that she was bearing up well in hospital and the surgeon was hopeful for a successful outcome for her, as he'd removed as much of the low-grade tumour as he could. Flora felt only slight relief from this news, knowing that her friend still had a long road ahead of her.

"So," the vicar continued, "hence my need to call this meeting. I have spoken with the Bishop and been granted a three month sabbatical to focus on my role as a husband and father. A new, temporary incumbent will be arriving in the village in a couple of weeks. Obviously, it would be very difficult for us to offer him a room in the vicarage at this time, so, ah, I was wondering, Flora, if…"

"No need to ask, of course he can stay at The Rise. Plenty of space there, and I'm thinking of hiring a housekeeper to keep the place ship shape," Flora answered, glad she could help in some small way.

"Perfect," James slumped back down into his chair, his black jacket already hanging more loosely on his slim frame, and coordinating with the dark circles under his eyes, "then that's everything…"

"Actually," a shrill voice cut in, "since we're all here I'd like to present a motion to have Mrs. Bramble-Miller removed from this council, and my husband seconds it!"

She prodded Doctor Edwards, who had been fiddling with his tie, and now muttered, "Yes, yes, whatever woman."

A collective gasp of shock rolled across the table.

"Now just a minute!" Adam said, as he and Harry both shot to their feet.

"Adam," Flora quickly interjected, standing up herself and glaring at the woman opposite her, "I can handle this. We were surprised, Edwina, to see you and Ernest here this evening, given your recent unexpected and frankly suspicious disappearance and then the police's interest in your alibis for the night of Minerva's murder. And that is even without the shame and embarrassment you must feel, Ernest," Flora deliberately chose to use their first names – any respect she once had for the couple was now long gone.

"We had a family emergency to attend to, and of course we have alibis! We are each other's alibi!" The screechy, high timbre of Edwina's voice was jarring and Flora felt her head begin to pound. "How about you, though, Mrs. Lady of the Manor, can you explain to the council why you felt the need to set my husband up as a sexual predator just to discredit him? Only a blind person wouldn't see that you want to get rid of anyone standing in your way of having full control of this village. Especially now that you've decided to buy out the parts of Baker's Rise that you don't own. I mean, you're even throwing money at the church to get your grubby feet under the ecumenical table! My husband has explained it all to me!"

"I'm sure he has," Flora said wryly.

"That's enough, Edwina," Harry spoke firmly, as Adam walked round to stand beside Flora.

"It's okay, Harry, I've got this. Edwina, I orchestrated no such thing, and well you know it. How convenient that Minerva is no longer here to confirm my words," Flora replied calmly, stretching to her full height, "though that is not to say that you're wrong in thinking your husband is discredited. He has, completely and irrevocably, lost any respect once held in this village. You both have in fact, and totally and utterly from your own doing. I hereby propose my own motion to have you both removed from the council. I would strongly urge you to reconsider your place in Baker's Rise, Ernest, as after hearing from several of our neighbours regarding their medical experiences with you , I do not believe you are required in a professional capacity any longer either."

"I second that motion," James said, his tired eyes bright with anger and levelled at Edwina, "let's put it to a vote."

Needless to say, the motion was carried unanimously and both of the Edwards couple had their names removed from the list of parish council representatives. Flora felt no remorse. She didn't dwell on the disgusting deed she had been accused of, knowing it was false in every sense. She also knew in her heart that she had offered money to save the church from a place of integrity with no desire for personal gain. The others on the council also believed, Flora was sure, that Edwina's claims were groundless.

The only ones whose characters had been further tarred by the accusations were the pair making them. Flora dearly hoped the couple would feel enough shame to leave the village with their tails between their legs.

The only remaining question was, would it be to a prison cell?

TWENTY-ONE

The weekend passed quietly, a fact for which Flora was very grateful. The weather seemed to have changed for the better, with a return to the crisp, bright autumn days that made a walk around the estate grounds a pleasure.

"Have you heard anything more from McArthur?" Flora asked as she and Adam strolled arm in arm around the ornamental gardens on Sunday afternoon, getting a bit of fresh air and exercise before a late lunch at Betty's.

"Only by text yesterday evening. She said that the doctor's wife apparently binned her costume the moment they arrived at the B&B where they were holing up, so Timpson is on the case going through Edwina's emails to find the online invoice so that he can source an exact replica from the same shop. Then it'll need to be tested, so not a quick answer to that literal loose end. Someone else on the investigation is going through Minerva's laptop, looking for any correspondence with her ex husband in case she taunted him with news of her upcoming tell-all publication. That would prove that he knew about the book and solidify the motive. All in all, still up in the air, love, but a few strong suspects so definitely on the right track."

"That's good, very good," Flora replied, her mind whirring, and wondering why she had brought up the topic in the first place. It only served to unsettle her all over again.

"I was thinking, Flora love... Quick, behind the bush!" Adam nudged her sideways, to Flora's surprise, and she was unfortunately too slow to get the hint.

"Flora! Adam! I tried the coach house and was hoping to find you up here. I may, ah, have annoyed the parrot with my shouting through the letterbox, though," Phil said, looking sheepish.

Great, Flora thought, *just when I'd managed to get Reggie calmed down with a sense of routine and normality again.*

To Phil she simply plastered on a smile, and wished she'd taken Adam's lead and jumped behind the nearest hedge to avoid being found.

"What did you want with us?" Adam asked, forgoing the usual obligatory chit chat.

"Well, ah, it's just that I've had your colleagues, ah ex-colleagues around, taking all my copies of sweet Minnie's book and quizzing me on whether she had any others, whom she'd sent the manuscript to and so on. I was wondering, Flora, if they might have had that tip off from you? It seems strange that they knew exactly what they missed when they searched and more so, exactly where to find it."

"I, ah, well, I…" Flora began, but Adam interrupted and answered for her.

"You will have told the detectives where you met Minerva, at the book fair, yes?" Adam asked, all business now.

"Erm, I did, yes."

"Well, then it wouldn't take much for them to assume she had a literary connection and to look into that, would it? I'm sure there are press photographs from that event in Carlisle, besides they have the deceased's laptop, which presumably contains the original drafts of the manuscript. And it isn't a great leap to assume books might be kept on a bookshelf since they were not in the other boxes and suitcases…" Adam raised an eyebrow at Phil who blushed and started stammering.

"Ah, y-yes, s-silly me, well it does seem obvious now you spell it out. Ah, Sorry Flora, sorry, I didn't mean to imply you had been reporting behind my back or anything…"

"Not to worry, Phil," Flora said, already turning to walk away, "bye for now."

They left the man standing where he was and continued their stroll, though Flora was in a bigger rush now as she knew she'd need to get Reggie settled before heading down to see Betty and Harry. She did have sympathy for Phil, of course, and felt slight guilt for telling McArthur about the book's contents, but it was nothing the police wouldn't have seen from Minerva's laptop anyway, as Adam had said. Flora was sure she had just expedited the process and pointed them in the right direction.

"Don't dwell on it, love," Adam said, as if he could read her mind, "you've done everything as you should have."

"Umhm," Flora mumbled, snuggling closer into her husband's side and wishing the whole sordid business would be done with once and for all.

She carried this determination to bring a swift resolution to the village's current troubles with her to Betty's later that day, having had no choice but to allow Reggie to accompany them. The bird's squawks of "Not that jerk!" and "The fool has arrived!" were still piercing the air when the couple returned to the coach house from their walk, and Flora had a few choice things to say about Phil when the parrot simply would not shut up. Grapes, blueberries, slices of banana… all provided only a temporary reprieve from his assault on her nerves. In the end, Flora had told Reggie that he could come out with them only if he silenced his beak. Whether the bird understood, or simply saw the carry case which Flora produced at the same time and put two and two together, Flora wasn't sure, but after a quick, "Adventure awaits!" a blissful quiet had fallen on the small cottage, just in time for them to go out again.

"Well, that was absolutely grand, Betty," Adam patted his full stomach and was on the receiving end of a girlish smile from their hostess.

"Oh get off with you!" Betty said, "It was just my normal Sunday fare." Her face, however, beamed with pleasure at the compliment and Flora noticed that her friend gave Adam two big scoops of trifle instead of one.

"Now, what did you want to ask me about, lass?" Harry asked when he and Adam had finished doing the dishes. Flora and Betty had shared a pot of tea and warmed themselves in the armchairs by the fire, little Tina and Reggie snoozing on their respective laps, so much so that Flora had pretty much dozed off by the time Harry had to say her name twice to get her attention.

"Hm? Oh! Sorry Harry," Flora jerked fully awake, suddenly remembering that she wasn't at home in the coach house and lowering her voice when she heard Betty's snoring, "sorry, yes, it was about the properties owned by the estate. Can we pop through to your study?"

The three of them crowded around Harry's computer as he pulled up the lists of homes and businesses with premises rented to them from the Baker's Rise estate.

"Is there any address in particular that you wish to check?" Harry asked, his old eyes curious.

"Actually, yes, can you tell me whether either the Edwards' home or the surgery building is owned by me?"

"Of course. I can tell you for a fact that the medical practice is in a building owned by the estate and their house…" Flora took a deep breath as she waited for his answer, "… no, the house is their own."

"Okay, well, that means we can't make them leave the village, but no matter, I can prevent him from continuing as village doctor. Please serve the medical practice with an end of lease notice, Harry, the shortest period that is legal."

"Are you sure?" Adam asked, and Flora regretted not mentioning her plan to him beforehand. There had seemed no point, however, until she learned whether she had any hold over the buildings used by the couple.

"Absolutely. James told me – in confidence, if you don't mind – that Sally had been to see Doctor Edwards over a month ago about her headaches and he brushed them off as the menopause without even examining her or taking a history. She's not even forty, for goodness sake!" Flora tried to tamp down her anger, "On top of all the other experiences that've been shared with me this week concerning the doctor's shockingly negligent approach, this was the final straw. I understand that being in my position is not all cosy tearooms and redecorating a manor house. No, it comes with a huge responsibility to my tenants and neighbours, and I'm ready to take on the full weight of that now."

"I'm so proud of you, Flora," Harry's eyes shone brightly, so much so that she caught a glimpse of the young man he had once been.

"And I too, love," Adam kissed her softly on the forehead, "so damn proud."

"What's all this then?" Betty asked, appearing bleary-eyed from the sitting room.

"Just our Flora becoming the woman she was always meant to be, taking on the mantle of leadership that she is perfectly cut-out for," Harry spoke as if she were their daughter, and Flora felt the praise settle in her heart and the warmth spread out to her bones.

"I told you, she just needed to get settled and let the village take root in her, the way it has with all of us," Betty said happily, "you were just what we needed, when we needed it, lass, and now you can see that too." Betty wiped away a happy tear and hugged Flora to her. Flora bent to accommodate the older woman's shorter frame and tried hard not cry.

There is family, and there is found family, and Flora knew she had finally found hers.

TWENTY-TWO

"You know they won't leave quietly, you may well have a fight on your hands," Adam said as they drove home.

"I know, and I'm ready for it," Flora said, meaning every word.

"Baker's Rise is very lucky to have you," her husband smiled and rubbed Flora's knee where she sat next to him, "but not as lucky as I am to have you as my wife."

"And I'm very blessed to have you and my neighbours… well, most of them," Flora replied, leaning over to kiss him on the temple, "one thing I did remember at Betty's though, you were about to tell me something when Phil appeared, what was it?"

"What? Oh, I, um," her husband seemed to suddenly lack the confidence to say what he was thinking, which was completely unlike him and so intrigued Flora even more. Clearly the subject was an important one, and one that Adam wasn't totally comfortable with, whatever it was.

"You can tell me anything, you know that," Flora said softly.

"I know love, it's um, well," the journey was such a short one, that they had pulled up outside of the coach house before Adam had managed to get his words out. Reggie was already desperate to get back out of his carry case and to dive into his seed bowl, so the conversation was put on hold until they were all snuggled up inside.

"So," Flora said when Adam had finished lighting the log burner and Reggie had given his approval for the conversation to continue, "So cosy!"

"So, ah," Adam sat down next to her on the sofa and took Flora's hands in his, "you know when we were looking after the Marshall girls last week?"

"Yes?" Flora suddenly wondered where he was going

with this, a frisson of excitement starting to build in her chest.

"Well, I mean, I know it was exhausting and we felt completely out of our depth, and all, but it got me thinking."

"In what way?" Flora didn't realise how much she'd wanted this conversation until now.

"Well, how nice it was to see the children enjoying the grounds at the big house, and to hear you playing hide and seek with them upstairs. Knowing we had brought them some joy in the midst of their family's difficult time."

"It was certainly all of those things," Flora could feel her heart beating quickly and had to stop herself from jumping the gun and pre-empting what her husband was about to say.

"So, I've been thinking love, since we had that heart to heart in the tearoom and then, as I say, since spending time with the girls… and I don't know anything about the process, I haven't read up on it at all as I wanted to get your opinion first, but, I mean, we could maybe look into fostering? We have the space up at The Rise if we were to move in there when any children needed us, and I have the time now and, I mean I didn't have a good family experience myself growing up and perhaps we could help another child to not feel the way I did…"

"Yes!" Flora threw her arms around his neck and squeezed, "Yes, yes, yes, let's do it! You're such a generous, kind man, Adam, in spite of your upbringing. Any child would be lucky to have you on their side."

"Right, okay then, that's great," Adam turned quite red and Flora couldn't tell if it was from emotion or from the tight hold she had around him.

"I've felt like I've been missing something for a while," Flora moved back slightly to give them both some breathing space, "but until recently I couldn't put my finger on it. I mean, look at everything I have here, and then getting married to you, my cup should've been overflowing with joy. And it was. Except for a small niggle that something was missing."

"I know, I've seen you struggle with it and since you planted that seed of thought… well, let's just say it's never been far from my mind," Adam paused and when he spoke again his voice was choked, "So, I'll get the ball rolling?"

"Absolutely, let's see what it involves and whether we

meet the criteria and then go from there," Flora's words sounded calm and measured now, but inside her heart was bursting and she wanted to shout their decision from the rooftops. It wasn't until Adam gently swiped his thumbs across her cheeks that Flora realised she was crying – happy tears for once!

"Silly bird!" Reggie muttered from his perch, seed husks stuck to his face feathers.

"I know, but she's my silly bird," Adam replied, hugging his wife to him.

TWENTY-THREE

October flowed into November without any changes other than the weather, which became decidedly colder. Flora was still shocked by the difference in temperature between here in the north of the country, and her years in London in the south. She brought out all of her thick knitwear from the previous winter, her many sets of decorated flannel pyjamas made a reappearance – even though she now had Adam to keep her warm – and the heating was always on in the tearoom to offer customers a warm welcome. Not so warm, was the letter she had received from Doctor Edwards' solicitor, refuting the eviction notice from the surgery premises. It was mainly bluster, however, as

Harry had assured her she was well within her legal right to request the property be returned to the estate after the four months obligatory notice period. Confident in her decision, but wary of a public showdown, Flora tended to avoid the centre of the village unless she had Adam or Tanya with her.

Nothing was heard about the investigation into Minerva's death, other than Adam telling Flora at the end of October that there hadn't been enough evidence to make an arrest. Both Rupert Strangelove and the Edwards couple had motive enough to want the woman dead, but the evidence couldn't be fully and irrevocably aligned with either suspect. Not according to the Crown Prosecution Service anyway. Flora disliked loose ends and unfinished business. All the more so when it involved a murderer still at large. That being said, she threw herself wholeheartedly into her work on the estate, into her newly elected role as chairwoman of the parish council, and into the friendships she had made. Not least of this, was organising a meal rota and childcare offers for the Marshall family while Sally underwent her follow-up treatment. So she had little spare time to ponder things that weren't her immediate concern, much to her husband's relief.

It was a cold but thankfully dry morning in late

November when Flora was sorting through the festive decorations ready to decorate the tearoom and bookshop the next week, when a very flustered Hilda May entered. Now, it was strange to see this elderly lady out and about without either Betty or one of her other W.I. friends. Even stranger, that the usually painfully shy woman was actively seeking Flora out. So, Flora set down the box she was currently sorting through and gave the woman her full attention.

The seconds ticked by and still Hilda said nothing, simply sitting down at the table nearest the door, her coat still on and her handbag clutched in both hands in front of her.

Looking from one to the other, Reggie decided to break the somewhat uncomfortable silence with a squawk of "You stupid old trout!" to which Flora scooped the bird from his perch in a swift, clandestine manoeuvre which he wasn't expecting, and sent him on his way through to Adam in the bookshop.

"Bad bird!" he shrieked as he was launched from her palms into the air, to which Flora simply tutted and turned her attention back to her customer.

"Hilda, how are you? Can I get you a pot of tea?"

"Tea?" Hilda looked up through her thick, wide-framed glasses, giving her the look of a rather startled owl, "Oh, I haven't collected my pension for this week yet."

"Oh! On the house then," Flora said, secretly hoping the woman hadn't come to discuss any financial difficulties. Since it had become public knowledge that Flora had 'saved' the church, she had been approached a few times for loans and monetary advice. Now she didn't mind helping out, but Flora didn't want to be the new Baker's Rise bank. She was keen to help the causes that she felt moved to support and to avoid any uncomfortable requests.

Joining Hilda at the table with a pot of Earl Grey and two slices of lemon drizzle cake, Flora twiddled the handle of her tea cup between her fingers until finally the older woman spoke up.

"Flora, I have a problem."

Flora nodded and waited, nodded and waited some more. Blew the steam from her tea and smiled encouragingly.

"It concerns the upcoming talent show." She was definitely a woman of few words.

Flora let out a silent sigh of relief at the subject of

Hilda's problem and affixed what she considered to be her most concerned, understanding expression, "Go on."

"Well, there was a sign-up sheet in the church hall. For refreshments for the evening, contributions to the cake stall, back stage help and so on, all over and above the actual participants taking part in the show. As you can imagine, I'm not talented in the performance area..."

Flora said nothing, simply nodded her understanding. To be honest, she'd have been shocked if Hilda was the performing type, but it would be impolite to say so.

"Anyway, there was a miscommunication. I thought Betty was signing up for us both, and she thought I was, and now... we've been left with the only job with no name against it, and to say Betty isn't pleased is an understatement." Hilda clasped her hands together on the table top and squeezed them tight. In an effort to calm her anxiety, Flora laid a hand on top of them.

"What job is that?" Flora asked.

"Marketing!" Hilda shrieked the word as if it was a dirty accusation and took a fortifying gulp of her sweet tea.

Flora tried hard not to smile, she could well imagine

Betty's reaction to that news, "Marketing as in posters?"

"Yes! And flyers and the programme for the evening… Betty is mad and I'm at a loss Flora. I don't know how to use the new technological magubbins."

"Well, Hilda, if it will help you out, Adam and I will take over that aspect of the production," Flora said, feeling to be honest as if she had got off lightly. She had been expecting to be called on to help with costumes or something else beyond her expertise, but this? This she could easily manage – with a little help from the printers in Alnwick.

"Really Flora? Oh my goodness! Thank you! Thank you! What shall I tell Betty?"

Flora understood that Hilda didn't want Betty to simply think she'd run straight to Flora telling tales so said, "Tell her that I had missed out on signing up and asked you if I could take the job from you in return for you both baking a few Christmas cake loaves for the tearoom."

"Flora you are an angel. Really, I can't tell you…" the gushing praise was extensive and embarrassing, and in the end Flora smiled, stood up and went back to sorting the decorations.

If only everyone in the village was this easily pleased!

TWENTY-FOUR

Flora and Adam had been sitting at the kitchen table for the past half an hour designing a draft mock-up of the poster for the talent show, to share with everyone for their approval at the rehearsal the following night.

"Have you got a headache love?" Adam asked rubbing Flora's shoulder in concern. He had shown more anxiety for his wife's health since Sally's illness and Flora understood, because it was a mutual worry. Having just found each other, they didn't want to lose their new life partner.

"No, ah, it's just that my mind won't stop whirring, I can't focus on this even though it's a simple task really."

"Where's you mind at?" Adam asked.

"Well, you won't be happy, but it's about Minerva's murder…"

Twenty minutes later they were both bundled up and on the way to Jean's flat above the shop.

"I hope it's not too late to call in," Flora worried as she pressed the doorbell.

"Too late now," Adam whispered, as they heard footsteps coming through the dark store and Jean's face appear in the window.

"It's just us," Flora called, trying to sound apologetic.

"Flora lass, and Adam, what a nice surprise," Jean invited them up and the couple were hit by a wall of heat as they entered the small living area.

"Smudge likes it tropical in here," Jean said, casting an indulgent look at the black and white cat sitting on a cat bed attached to the top of the radiator. In return, he gave them all a dismissive glare and turned his face back to the wall.

"He's friendly," Adam whispered sarcastically, earning him a nudge in the ribs from Flora.

"So, shall we have chocolate cake and tea? Or would you prefer coffee, Adam?"

"Oh, tea is fine," Adam said, eying the huge chocolate cake which sat on the counter in the open-plan room. They had not long eaten dinner, but by the hungry look in her husband's eyes you'd think he hadn't eaten for a week.

Flora gave him an expression which she hoped conveyed 'really?' and then asked after Jean's family, hoping to dispose of the pleasantries as quickly as possible, as they had the farm to get to next.

"Well, Phoebe and Lachlan are engaged! You remember Phoebe don't you?"

Flora wondered how she could possibly forget, memories of her murderous former gardener and his womanizing ways flitting though her mind, "Yes, of course, oh how lovely."

"Yes, and my sister is thrilled, of course. There was a time she thought Phoebe would go right off the rails, cheeky wee miss that she was…"

Ten minutes later and Adam was accepting his second

huge slab of cake. Flora decided to speed things up a bit, "So, ah Jean, the reason for our visit, I mean was to catch up on your news of course, but we actually needed to ask you a question about the night of the Autumn Fayre, since you stayed the night at the farm whereas Lily and I came to help with the birth."

"Aye lass, I remember, now what is it you need to know?"

"It's about who was in the farmhouse, if you can recall – or rather, who perhaps wasn't…"

"Well, that was enlightening," Flora said as they bundled back into the car and made their way to the Houghton's farm.

"Hmm maybe," Adam clearly preferred to reserve judgement until they had all the facts, and Flora understood his reticence, "are you sure Lily won't mind? It's after nine."

"No, I just texted her and she said if we don't mind the vision of her in her nightwear then we're welcome."

"Glorious," Adam replied, the sarcasm positively dripping from his tone now.

"So, are you sure you don't want tea?" Lily whispered over the snores of her husband, who was asleep on his chair by the fire, Bertie by his feet. Refusing a hot drink on a social visit in Baker's Rise was akin to not curtseying before royalty – rude and unheard of.

"No thanks, it's just a quick visit," Flora answered swiftly, as Adam eyed the banana loaf that sat on a cooling rack on the table in front of them, "I was wondering if you have any photos from the night of the fayre? Of people in their costumes?"

"Well, as you can imagine most of the stuff left over was taken by the police, even all my jars of jam that were in the barn with the barrel and the body…" Lily shuddered and tightened the belt on her dressing gown, "but I have some pictures on my phone that I took when the event was all set up, before the families arrived. You might see who you're looking for in one of those?"

"Perfect," Flora smiled as Lily searched through her phone, her hands shaking slightly as she relived the memories of that first week of the police investigation.

"It must've been very hard up here, Lily," Adam said gently, "having so many strangers tramping around, and then not able to let customers up to the farm shop and everything."

"Aye," Lily paused her scrolling, lowering her voice even further, "actually it's been awful to tell you the truth. The dairy farming is a part of our income, but we rely on the farm shop to sell the cheese and butter we make, and on the sales of my baked goods, jams and chutneys to top us up. Now, even though we're back open, no one wants to visit us up here, we've got a black mark against our name in the locals' minds."

"Oh Lily, I'm so sorry, I didn't think," Flora felt awful for not checking on her friend recently, she tapped her finger on the table in thought, "you need a solution, before the Christmas trade. I remember those lovely hampers you made up last year."

"Aye but what?" Lily's eyes looked suspiciously watery and Flora rubbed her friend's shoulder gently.

"The old Jones bakery shop is empty, isn't it Flora?" Adam asked, "And owned by the Baker's estate?"

"It is!" Flora replied excitedly, seeing where he was going with this, "And you were already outgrowing that small outbuilding you'd converted, Lily, how about you take the leap and set up a proper shop in the village? You'd get more custom because people wouldn't have to trek up here, and I'd even give you the first three months' rent free."

"Oh my goodness!" Lily's hands cradled her red cheeks and her wide eyes shone with hope for the first time since they'd arrived, "Do you really think I could do it?"

"Absolutely," they both answered in unison.

"Like Baker's Rise Farm Fresh Supplies? Or something?"

"Well, you know what, some traditions are best kept and others..? Change can be healthy. How about something simple like Lily's Farm Shop?" Flora said, having always thought the rhyming names were a bit silly.

"I'll talk to Stan in the morning, but basically the man does what I tell him, and he'll be all for a bit more money so we're not stretched as tight... oh here are the photos," she handed the phone over as an afterthought.

Flora flicked through the pictures quickly, Adam leaning over her shoulder. They were mainly of the barrel of jam, of the tractor and trailer strung with fairy lights, of Lily in her outfit in front of a mirror, of the chocolate stall, and "Bingo!" Flora declared.

"Find what you needed?" Lily asked distractedly, not

even bothering to enquire who Flora had been looking for.

"I did indeed," Flora said triumphantly, zooming in on the figure in the background of the photo and screenshotting the image before sending it across to her own email account.

Two down, one to go, but the largest piece of the puzzle would have to wait until tomorrow.

TWENTY-FIVE

Flora was on tenterhooks until Tanya arrived to take over from her and Adam the next morning. She had burnt a dozen scones and scolded Reggie for trying to take a mouthful of the charred remains. Not one to be dissuaded, the little bird threw the chunk at Flora instead, pretending that had been his mission all along. Needless to say, this did not help her mood.

"Now, love," Adam said cautiously, a man walking on egg shells if ever there were one, "now love, don't be getting yourself in a tizz. I know that working on the posters and programme sent your head a-whumping or whatever it is…"

"Whirring," Flora said flatly.

"Yes, exactly, ah, a-whirring, and I know the other information we got last night supports your theory, but that's all it is, a theory. No need to get het up," he paused as Flora locked him with squinted, angry slits for eyes and quickly rephrased, "ah, I mean concerned, but let's not jump the gun, eh love?"

"Who's jumping over guns?" Tanya asked, waltzing in in a flurry of leopard print and faux fur.

"No one," Flora muttered, grabbing her handbag from under the counter, and levelling her steely glare on the parrot who had just landed on her friend's shoulder, "and you be good, Reginald Parrot, or grapes are off the menu!"

"Silly old trout! Bad bird!" The litany of name calling followed the couple from the shop and out into the brisk air.

It was a rather hungover Phil who answered the door to them, acting as if it were seven in the morning and not the very respectable hour of ten. Flora was not to be put off, however, seeing as she was a woman on a mission, and Adam could only shrug his shoulders and mouth 'sorry' silently from behind her as she strode past Phil and into his sitting room. If she had thought the room a sight before, it had nothing on the empty lager cans and cheap vodka bottles, the take-out cartons and dirty dishes that Flora now waded through, quickly giving up on the hope of finding a spot to perch on the litter-strewn sofa.

"Phil, it makes me sad to see you living like this," Flora said gently.

"If the state of the place bothers you, from a landlady point of view, then just evict me," the man said, his voice devoid of any fight.

"What? No, I meant for your sake, um, how can we help you?"

"Get me Minerva back."

"Okay, ah, perhaps I can rally some of the men to help Phil do a tidy up and get him a haircut and a good shave later in the week," Adam interjected, clearly keen to get this over with, "but in the meantime, mate, would you mind if Flora takes a look at Minerva's scrapbooks?"

"What? So you can tell the coppers and have these taken away from me too?" Phil's voice had found a certain vehemence now, and Adam stepped between him and Flora.

"No, no, just want to check one quick thing. No reporting back to anybody," Flora said.

"Absolutely not," for being tired and probably still inebriated, the man was resolute now.

"What if it might lead to Minerva's killer being caught and punished?" Adam asked, trying a different tactic.

Phil seemed to weigh this up, a cold smile forming as he replied, "Only if I get an hour in a locked room with them before the police are called."

"I can't agree to that," Adam said quickly, when it felt like Flora was about to cave, "but don't you want justice for the woman you love?"

"It won't bring her back," Phil said, his voice childlike and desperate now.

"No, but it might give you some closure," Flora stepped forward and pointed to the large scrapbooks which lay open on the carpet under the window, where Phil had obviously been going through them, "one look, Phil, please, you owe her that much."

To the couple's surprise, the man in question seemed to crumple before them then, with Adam only just catching him in time before Phil staggered backwards towards the unlit fireplace. Sobs wracked his body and he looked like he might be sick. Adam gave Flora a look of 'now look what we've done' and helped Phil through to the kitchen.

"Come on, mate, let's make a cup of coffee and see what food you've got in, we're not going to leave you in this state."

Flora paused for only a moment before her decision was made. Rushing across the room and crouching down, she flicked quickly through the top scrapbook, realised it was not the one she had looked through previously and discarded it gently, picking up the next in the pile.

This is it, she thought, the pictures of a younger Minerva triggering her memory as Flora turned page after page until she found what she was looking for. There it was, a twenty-year-old show programme from Stratford-upon-Avon, with a group photo of the whole cast as the centre pages. Flora fumbled around in her bag for her mobile phone and took some quick pictures. She didn't dare take the actual booklet itself for fear Phil would notice it missing. If this all came to nothing, then it was pointless upsetting the man further for no reason. She hurried through to the kitchen as nonchalantly as possible and was touched to see her husband washing the dishes whilst the kettle boiled. He gave her a quick sideways, questioning glance and Flora nodded once, before joining him at the counter and adding instant coffee granules to the cups he'd just dried.

"We'll have to have it black as you've got no milk. I'll call round later with some groceries," Flora said gently, handing Phil the mug. He seemed better composed now, thankfully, "Let us, let the village help you through this. Maybe come along to the tearoom for a chat or visit the manor house and meet the new stand-in vicar, he seems lovely. Anything really, so that you get out of the house and are not so lonely."

"She's right, mate, sometimes you have to lean in on the people who want to help you."

"I'll see," Phil said, and Flora knew that was as much as they'd get for today.

"It'll have to be tonight, in the church hall before the rehearsal, catch them unawares and in a public place," Adam said, studying the photo as soon as they were back in the car, "I'll phone McArthur and make some arrangements."

"Righty-o," Flora replied, a shiver running up her

spine – whether from excitement or fear she wasn't sure.

If she'd got it wrong, then it would only be herself embarrassed in front of most of the village. If she was right though, a murderer who would've otherwise gone undetected would be caught.

It was worth the risk.

TWENTY-SIX

Flora wiped her clammy hands on her warm winter trousers and flicked her hair nervously. It was now or never.

"Are you sure you want to go in there?" Tanya asked, appearing behind her in the corridor next to the kitchen in the chilly church hall, "Edwina's there, throwing her weight about as if she and her husband haven't been disgraced in front of the whole village."

Since her friend didn't know the real reason for Flora's visit – believing instead that she had brought the marketing images for approval – Flora simply offered her a weak smile and said, "I'll have to brave it."

They walked together through the wooden door which separated the main hall from the rest of the building, Flora noticing for the first time how the old, brown paint was peeling and the handle broken. She felt hyperaware of her surroundings, and was glad she'd left Reggie at the coach house so he couldn't pick up on her tension.

The hall was a bustle of activity, with sets being painted, carols being practised on the out-of-tune piano, and one single performer practicing up on the stage.

"Bunny," Flora raised her voice to be heard from where she had positioned herself on the scuffed parquet floor in the middle of the room, needing two attempts to catch the woman's attention, so engrossed was she in the soliloquy she was acting.

How apt that she's reciting the words of Iago from 'Othello' and not something more Christmassy, Flora thought, as all around her came to an abrupt halt and a heavy silence blanketed them. Flora could feel a dozen pairs of eyes on her, and had to force herself to stand her ground in front of them all.

"Strange choice," Flora shocked herself by ditching her prepared speech and going with the first thing in her mind, "a speech by a Machiavellian schemer, overcome by obsession and bent on destruction of the one who wronged them. Yet so apt, when you think about it."

"What do you mean?" Bunny's initial smile of welcome had been swiftly replaced by a wary stare.

"I think you know. But for the benefit of our audience, let me explain," Flora said, her voice strong and confident, despite the shaking in her legs, "You see everyone, Bunny here met the recently departed Minerva long before their chance encounter in the pub last month. Twenty years ago in fact, when they both performed in the same play down south. But Minerva had the starring role, didn't she, Bunny? And you were merely in the chorus. Some sort of lumberjack?"

Bunny stood silently, clearly weighing up her options.

"Go on then, tell us the story," Betty urged, taking a seat at the side of the hall and getting comfortable for the show, even laying down her knitting.

"Well, I'm sure Ms. Hopper here will enlighten us, but I'd suggest she wanted that main role for herself, but wasn't up to scratch. Not any competition for the talented Minerva," Flora was deliberately goading now, "and has had a chip on her shoulder ever since, following her career from an increasingly envious distance. I'm sure there are even photos of Bunny in

the audience at some of Minerva's burlesque shows."
The last was a guess, but Flora was going with it.

Flora paused and all eyes turned to Bunny to either
corroborate or dispute the assumptions. If she had to
describe the woman who towered over her on the stage
now, Flora would have likened her to a pot about to
boil over, steam and all.

"Pathetic. That's what she was," Bunny spat the words,
"using her wily ways to buy her the part. She knew
fine well what her only real asset was," Bunny
clenched her jaw shut firmly to prevent herself from
saying anything else.

"Are you claiming Minerva got that part two decades
ago by egregious means?" Flora asked.

"She used her body to buy that part as she always did
before and since," Bunny blurted out, to shocked gasps
from those assembled.

"And you would have been given it otherwise?" Flora
used her most incredulous tone.

"Of course, any fool could see the difference in talent
between the two of us. But what did I get? Woodcutter
number two," she waggled her broad shoulders and
jutted her head forwards in such a way as to appear

threatening and Flora spared a quick glance to the wings of the stage. The woman seemed almost deranged, and Flora hadn't even got into the specifics of the Autumn Fayre yet. She wondered if she should let the professionals do the rest.

"Go on," Betty urged her, all but getting out a box of popcorn from her handbag.

"On the night of Minerva's death you wore a spider costume," Flora decided to move this on quickly.

"That's not a crime, nor is it news," Bunny's nostrils flared as her uber-confidence returned.

"No, however I'd be surprised if the rough cotton webbing that you wore as a shawl didn't come back as a match for the thread's caught on the back of the victim's dress," Flora refused to step back as the woman on the stage moved to its very edge, poised to jump off, "I have a photo from that evening showing you from behind, and the fake spider's web is clear from that angle. Moreover, you were the only one of the original helpers not present in the farmhouse during the storm later that evening. Why did you take off so suddenly, if not because you had just murdered the woman you always blamed for taking the part that you believed would have launched your acting career? The woman that you had lost track of, only to find again after a chance meeting in a little country pub in rural Northumberland, where she had landed on her feet yet again. I can only imagine the feelings that brought back. Murderous ones, evidently."

"You have no proof," Bunny shouted, causing Hilda May to gasp and shield her face, whilst Betty sat beside her enthralled.

"The cotton fibres will be evidence, as will your phone history which the police will want to see – I mean, how did Minerva's estranged husband find her here, if not from a tip-off? No doubt from someone wanting her to get her just desserts. Besides, I'm sure you have a pretty interesting internet history and some rather incriminating files on your computer from following Minerva, maybe even trolling her over the years. Police officers have a warrant and are currently searching your flat," Flora took a deep breath to a round of applause from the villagers.

Not taking her eyes off the bullish woman who actually roared at her now across the space between them, charging the air with an almost electric current of desperation and fury, Flora watched as Adam, McArthur and Timpson emerged from the curtains on either side of the stage and restrained the woman who was about to charge forwards off the raised platform.

It all happened so fast, and yet in strangely slow motion. One minute Bunny was fighting her captors, arms and legs flailing and an almost inhuman noise coming from her, and the next she had been removed from the stage and the room fell into a deathly silence.

"Well, that was better than Edwina and her awful opera attempts," Betty declared, despite the woman herself being in the room as well.

Flora began to laugh at that, and once she started she couldn't stop. Then there were tears rolling down her face, as the adrenaline and relief still coursed through her body.

"All alright, love?" Adam asked, concern etched into the wrinkles in his forehead as he hurried back to her.

"Yes, just, ah, well, just Baker's Rise," and funnily he seemed to know exactly what she meant!

TWENTY-SEVEN

"And this all came out at the rehearsal for Baker's Rise Stars in Their Eyes the other night?" Sally leant forwards where she was cosied up on the sofa in the vicarage living room, under a pretty, crocheted blanket. She was surrounded by potted plants, flowers and homemade gifts which the villagers brought round regularly to remind her she was still in their hearts.

"It did, well, I mean, Adam and I had done a small bit of undercover investigating first," Flora blushed and took a sip of her tea.

"Well, thank goodness for that. And to think she has been teaching our children!"

"Yes, according to the statement she gave the detectives, teaching was a fallback career and one which Bunny hated. She would have slipped through safeguarding checks, though, as up till now she's never done anything to bring her to the attention of the police."

"I'm thankful they've caught her, that's for sure. What a lovely idea for Lily to open the shop, she texted me all excited the other morning."

"I know, and I wish we'd thought of it sooner. Never mind, she'll be set up in time for the Christmas rush, Adam and I will make sure of it."

"So kind of you, Flora," Sally yawned and Flora could tell her friend was nearing her conversational limit just as the front door burst open and pandemonium was let loose in the hallway.

Flora rose to find out the cause of the ruckus, though she had a very good idea who it would be, "Girls, girls, quietly now your mum is resting." Flora smiled at Rosa, Matias and Laurie who had followed the three exuberant youngsters in.

"Look Mummy! I made you a picture," Megan held up a painting which dripped slowly onto the polished wooden floor, a mixed media affair which had feathers and glitter stuck to the brightly coloured paint seemingly at random.

"Well, that is very special. Another to be proudly displayed on the fridge," Sally said, surreptitiously handing the collage to Flora when her daughter ran off to hang up her coat.

"I'll be getting along," Flora said, "I need a word with Laurie and Rosa here."

They said their goodbyes and Flora sent up a silent prayer of thanks that her friend was looking better than she had since before the operation. *Definitely on the mend,* she hoped.

"Was it something I've missed up at the big house?" Laurie asked as the four walked back past the village green.

"Not at all, it's something more personal actually. I don't know if you've heard, I mean it is like living in a goldfish bowl so I never expect anything to stay private for long, but, ah, Adam and I have decided to register for fostering. We've been to an introduction evening with other hopeful fosterers, filled in lots of forms, had our first face to face meeting… anyway, that's my roundabout way of saying that I've been thinking about growing our family, and I know you're trying to grow yours, so I've got this for you," Flora felt her cheeks heating as she hunted in her handbag for the envelope. She was wishing now that they'd had this conversation over a cuppa at the coach house, but it was too late to start afresh now.

Laurie opened the envelope in silence, read the contents and then handed it to Rosa without a word.

"What's this?" the young woman choked out.

"An early Christmas bonus," Flora felt the butterflies taking flight in her stomach now, hoping her gesture would be taken in the way it was intended, "for, ah, for the IVF you need to grow you family, Laurie, ah, mentioned…"

Flora was caught off guard as Rosa enveloped her in a tight hug.

"Thank you, Flora, gracias, gracias, gracias."

Laurie still seemed unable to form words. His eyes shone brightly and he clasped Flora's hand and squeezed it tight.

"We're family up at The Rise," Flora whispered around the lump in her own throat, "we look out for each other."

When Flora arrived back at the tearoom it was almost time to close up for the day. She said a passing hello to the new vicar, Christopher Cartwright, as he left the shop with her new housekeeper, Genevieve. The pair seemed to be getting on very well, Flora noted with relief, since they had both moved into The Rise in the same week. From what she could tell, they were both quiet souls with a shared love of books and the outdoors.

No doubt Betty will have her matchmaking hat on before too long, Flora thought wryly as she was greeted by shrieks of "You sexy beast!"

On entering the tearoom fully, however, Flora saw that the moniker was not aimed at her, but rather had been directed at a very red-faced Detective Timpson, who seemed to be trying to hide behind his coffee mug as Reggie assailed him with his rudest phrases, no doubt enjoying the reaction he was getting.

McArthur could no longer hide her sniggers behind her hand and began laughing outright, whilst even Adam had a chuckle.

"He's been on top form while I've been out, I see," Flora noted.

"Indeed love, and you'll be happy to know Hopper has been formally charged, and the search I asked McArthur to do on the new vicar has come back clean."

"Really, Adam, you can't be getting your former colleagues to do background checks on everyone who moves into the village!"

"I can when they're living in our house, where we'll hopefully be looking after children sometime next year."

"True, true," Flora accepted his kiss on the cheek and stroked the soft feathers of the little parrot who had settled on her shoulder, "we've got a lot to look forward to, here's hoping it's smooth sailing from now on."

Will Flora and Adam be sailing smoothly into their future together, or will there be more murder and mischief afoot in Baker's Rise?

*Join Flora and Reggie in, "**Things Cannoli Get Better,**" the ninth instalment in the Baker's Rise Mysteries series.*

A cosy new series is out now featuring Reverend Daisy Bloom and her rather secretive neighbours.

*"**Fresh as a Daisy,**" the first instalment in the **Lillymouth Mysteries** series set in North Yorkshire*

Read on for an excerpt…

.

AN EXCERPT FROM *FRESH AS A DAISY – THE LILLYMOUTH MYSTERIES BOOK ONE*

Daisy Bloom hummed along to the Abba song on Smooth radio, pondering how she might use the lyric 'knowing me, knowing you' this coming Sunday, in the first sermon she would deliver in her new parish. She was barely concentrating on her driving in fact, knowing the roads like the back of her hand as she did. Barely anything changed around here, in this small coastal corner of Yorkshire, and Daisy really wasn't sure if that was a good thing or not. It had been fifteen years since she had left the town of Lillymouth, at the tender age of eighteen, and the newly ordained vicar had not been back since. Indeed, had the Bishop himself not personally decreed this was the parish for her – in some misguided attempt to help her chase away the demons of her past, Daisy presumed – then she suspected that she would not have come back now either.

Positives, think about the positives, Daisy told herself, pushing a finger between her dog collar and her neck to let a bit of air in. The weather was remarkably lovely for early July in the North of England, and Daisy was regretting wearing the item which designated her as a member of the clergy. She had wanted to arrive at her new vicarage with no possibility that they not immediately recognise her as the new incumbent – after that awful time when she turned up as the curate of her last parish, and they had mistaken her as the new church organist. Not helped by the fact that she was tone deaf… She knew she looked very different from the fresh-faced girl who had left town under a black cloud though, so there was a good chance even the older townsfolk wouldn't recognise her.

Anyway, positive thoughts, positive thoughts, Daisy allowed her mind to wander to the shining light, the beacon of hope for her return to this little town – her new goddaughter and namesake, Daisy Mae, daughter of her best friend from high school, Bea. Pulling up outside of the bookshop which her friend owned, and glad to have found a disabled parking spot so close,

Daisy was surprised to find she was relieved that the old Victorian building had not changed since she left all those years ago. It still stood tall and proud on the bottom corner of Cobble Wynd and Front Street, it's wooden façade hinting at its age. The building had been a bookshop since Edwardian times, Daisy knew, and she smiled as she saw the window display was filled with baby books and toys – old and new coming together in harmony, something that, according to the Bishop, was far from happening in the town as a whole.

"Daisy!" the familiar voice brought a sudden lump to her throat as Daisy made her way into the relative dimness of the shop, the smell of books and coffee a welcome comfort. The voice of the woman who had been her childhood friend, who had been one of the few to support her when the worst happened all those years ago... *positive thoughts...*

"Bea," Daisy leant her walking stick against the old wooden counter and reached out to hug her friend, careful that her own ample bosom didn't squash the little baby that was held in a carrier at her mother's chest. Wanting to say more, but finding herself unable to speak around her emotion, Daisy tried to put all of the love and affection she could into that physical touch.

"Meet Daisy Mae," Bea said proudly, pulling back and turning sideways so that Daisy could see the baby's face.

"The photos didn't do her justice, Bea, really, she's beautiful." Okay, now the feelings had gone to her eyes, and Daisy tried to wipe them discreetly with the back of her hand. She wasn't this person, who was so easily moved – or at least she hadn't been since she ran and left Lillymouth behind. Daisy had funded herself through training and then worked as a police support officer for victims of violence for almost a decade, before hearing the calling to serve a higher purpose. She had survived assault and injury as part of her previous profession, seen some truly horrible things, and yet had not felt as emotional as she did now. Not since the day she quit this place, in fact…

"Aw, you must be tired from the drive," Bea, tactful and sensitive as always, gave her the perfect 'out', "come and have a cuppa and a sandwich in the tea nook. Andrew just finished refurbishing it for me."

"Thank you, but let me get it for you, are you even meant to be working so soon after the birth?"

"I'm just covering lunchtimes while my maternity cover nips out for a quick bite – well, I think she's actually meeting her boyfriend, she never manages to stick to just the one hour, but, ah, she's young and well read… why don't you hold little Daisy while I get us sorted with something?"

"Oh! I… well, I…"

"You'll be fine, Daisy, you're going to have a lot of babies to hold during christenings, you know! I can't wait for you to christen this little one," Bea chuckled and unfastened the baby pouch, handing the now squirming bundle to the vicar without hesitation once Daisy had lowered herself into a squashy leather armchair.

Wide, deep blue eyes, the colour of the swell in Lillywater Bay on a stormy day looked up at Daisy with surprise and she found herself saying a quick prayer that the baby wouldn't start to scream. Daisy desperately wanted to be a part of this little girl's life, feeling as she did that she might never have a child of her own. What she had seen in her previous profession had put Daisy off relationships for life. As part of the Church of England she was not forbidden from getting married and starting a family – quite the opposite – but Daisy's own feelings on the matter ran deep and dark.

"Here we go," Bea returned with a tray holding a pot

of tea, two china mugs, a plate of sandwiches and some cakes, "you look like you could do with this."

"You aren't wrong there," Daisy felt suddenly and surprisingly bereft as baby Daisy Mae was lifted gently from her arms and placed in a pram in the corner next to them.

"Have you visited the vicarage yet? Nora will be on tenterhooks waiting for you, she'll have Arthur fixing and cleaning everything, poor man!"

"I haven't had that pleasure," Daisy smiled ruefully, "I thought I'd come to visit my two favourites first," Daisy smiled back, knowing she was being slightly cowardly, but Nora Clumping was not a woman to become reacquainted with on an empty stomach. She had been the housekeeper at the vicarage for as long as Daisy could remember, surviving numerous clergy, and she had seemed ancient to Daisy as a girl. She could only imagine how old the woman must be now. She must have a soft side though, Daisy had thought to herself on the journey from Leeds, otherwise she wouldn't have taken Arthur in decades ago and adopted him as her own. Not that that diminished from the woman's formidable presence, however... for someone so slight in stature, she was certainly a powerhouse to contend with!

"Ah, wise choice," Bea agreed, "and if I were you, I'd pick up some fruit scones from Barnes the Baker's before you head up there!"

"Sound advice," Daisy laughed out loud, before remembering the baby who had now fallen back asleep, and lowered her voice to a whisper to joke, "I may be in the church now, but I'm not above the odd bit of bribery where necessary!"

"Just wait till you hear her views on the previous vicar," Bea said, not a small amount of excitement in her voice, "oh how I wish I could be a fly on the wall!"

"Argh," Daisy groaned exaggeratedly into her coffee mug causing her friend to snort.

"I want all the details afterwards," Bea continued, "I'll bet you five pounds that within ten minutes she mentions that time she caught you making a daisy chain with flowers you'd pulled from the vicarage garden."

"I was eight!" Daisy replied in mock protest, even while still knowing her friend was right – nothing was ever forgotten in small towns like these.

"Well, I've still got your back like I did then," Bea said, reaching over to rub Daisy's shoulder conspiratorially, and adding with a wink, "and I'm sure she isn't allowed to give the new vicar chores as punishment!"

Perhaps coming back to this place after so long won't be so bad after all, Daisy thought. *With good friends like this, I can serve the parish, find the justice I seek for Gran and be out of here before the Bishop can say 'Amen.'*

The Bible says 'seek ye first the Kingdom of God' – well, I've done that, now I can seek out a cold hearted killer. They may have gotten away with it for over a decade, but divine retribution is about to be served.

Things Cannoli Get Better

Baker's Rise Mysteries Book Nine

Publication Date: 19ᵗʰ May 2023

The scene is set, the cast assembles for a summer soiree to die for – quite literally in this case.

When Flora decides to hire a Murder Mystery troupe to bring a touch of Italian glamour to The Rise, she intends to transport her guests to the Amalfi coast for an evening of spritz and sleuthing.

Never ones to turn down an opportunity for eccentric excitement, the villagers transform themselves…
Movie stars, mobsters, even a motor racing legend.

It's all fun and games until someone is actually murdered.

Of course, it wouldn't be Baker's Rise without Reggie wanting a pizza the action, or several puns that are decidedly pasta their sell by date!

Packed with twists and turns, colourful characters and a splash of glitz and glamour, this new mystery will certainly leave you hungry for more!

Fresh as a Daisy

The Lillymouth Mysteries Book One

Coming February 17ᵗʰ 2023

A new mystery series from R. A. Hutchins, author of the popular Baker's Rise Mysteries, combines the charm of a Yorkshire seaside town with the many secrets held by its inhabitants to produce a delightful, cosy page-turner.

When Reverend Daisy Bloom is appointed to the parish of Lillymouth she is far from happy with the decision. Arriving to find a dead body in the church grounds, leaves her even less so.

Reacquainting herself with the painful memories of her childhood home whilst trying to make a fresh start, Daisy leans on old friends and new companions. Playing the part of amateur sleuth was never in her plan, but needs must if she is to ever focus on her own agenda.

Are her new neighbours all as they seem, or are they harbouring secrets which may be their own undoing? Worse still, will they also lead to Daisy's demise?

A tale of homecoming and homicide, of suspense and secrets, this is the first book in the Lillymouth Mysteries Series.

Available for pre-order now!

ABOUT THE AUTHOR

Rachel Hutchins lives in northeast England with her husband, three children and their dog Boudicca. She loves writing both mysteries and romances, and enjoys reading these genres too! Her favourite place is walking along the local coastline, with a coffee and some cake!

You can connect with Rachel and sign up to her monthly **newsletter** via her website at: www.authorrachelhutchins.com

Alternatively, she has social media pages on:

Facebook: www.facebook.com/rahutchinsauthor

Instagram: www.instagram.com/ra_hutchins_author

OTHER BOOKS BY R. A. HUTCHINS

The Angel and the Wolf

What do a beautiful recluse, a well-trained husky, and a middle-aged biker have in common?
Find out in this poignant story of love and hope!

When Isaac meets the Angel and her Wolf, he's unsure whether he's in Hell or Heaven.
Worse still, he can't remember taking that final step.
They say that calm follows the storm, but will that be the case for Isaac?

Fate has led him to her door,
Will she have the courage to let him in?

To Catch A Feather
Found in Fife Book One

When tragedy strikes an already vulnerable Kate Winters, she retreats into herself, broken and beaten. Existing rather than living, she makes a journey North to try to find herself, or maybe just looking for some sort of closure.

Cameron McAllister has known his own share of grief and love lost. His son, Josh, is now his only priority. In his forties and running a small coffee shop in a tiny Scottish fishing village, Cal knows he is unlikely to find love again.

When the two meet and sparks fly, can they overcome their past losses and move on towards a shared future, or are the memories which haunt them still too real?

These books, as well as others by Rachel, can be found on Amazon worldwide in e-book and paperback formats, as well as free to read on Kindle Unlimited.

Printed in Great Britain
by Amazon